Concho Folks

Tatiana,
All my best!
Pam Backlund 2020

Concho Folks

Volume 1

Pam Backlund

River Avenue Press
San Angelo, Texas

Concho Folks Volume 1
1800s Fictional Short Stories
Copyright © 2020 by Pam Backlund

For permission requests, write to the publisher at http://www.pamsliterature.com for ordering information. There are discounts on large quantities of orders for US trade bookstores and wholesalers. For details, contact the publisher at the address above.

Interior illustrations by Pam Backlund
Cover illustration and design by Katie Risor
https://www.katierisor.com/
Interior design by John Osterhout http://johnosterhout.com

ISBN 978-1-7345776-0-0 (paper)
     978-1-7345776-1-7 (ebook)
LCCN 2020902175

   1. Main category— Historical Fiction American / Treatises and
      Collections / Short Story
   2. Other category—American Fiction / Short Stories / Historical

River Avenue Press
San Angelo, Texas
First Edition 2020

I am deeply indebted to my loving, wise and witty husband, Bruce Backlund. I also dedicate this book to all my friends and family who have supported me through the years.

CONTENTS

Contents

Contents

Important:
San Angel*o*, north of Fort Concho was called San Angel*a* until 1884.

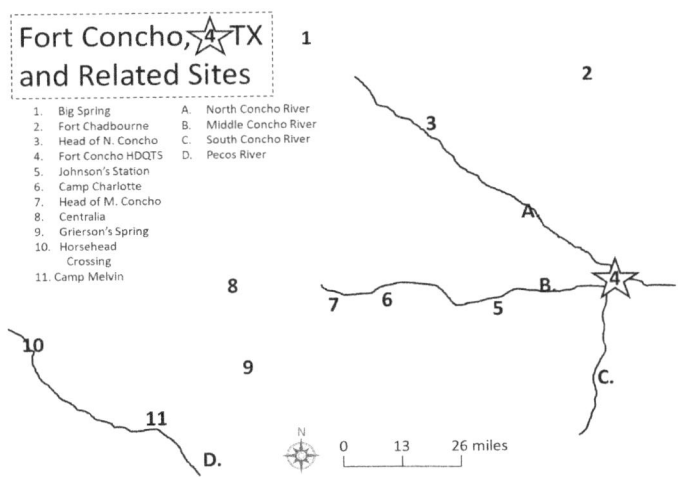

Fort Concho, ☆ TX and Related Sites

1. Big Spring
2. Fort Chadbourne
3. Head of N. Concho
4. Fort Concho HDQTS
5. Johnson's Station
6. Camp Charlotte
7. Head of M. Concho
8. Centralia
9. Grierson's Spring
10. Horsehead Crossing
11. Camp Melvin

A. North Concho River
B. Middle Concho River
C. South Concho River
D. Pecos River

0   13   26 miles

The author traced this map from the book:
Standing in the Gap by Loyd M. Uglo, page 130.

CHAPTER 1

1878 Shoulder Buddies

*L*ife is tiring; but at least we get a salary. That was the motto of the Camp Charlotte regiment. Their tough roadwork job was secure because no one else at Fort Concho wanted it. Soldiers, such as Bram, were shortening road lengths and fixing damaged lanes to Head of Middle Concho. The soldiers reduced travel time to the western parts of the district by straightening curvy routes.

For the privates, two months of work at Camp Charlotte equated to twenty-six dollars in greenbacks or—because of the exchange rate—twenty dollars in silver coins.

Private Bram (short for Abram) was from Virginia. His momma was still there awaiting his money; to travel to Texas. But it wasn't easy making currency for his momma. He had become handicapped while on a job at the fort.

Recently, Bram's leg had become permanently injured. He could walk, but he was slow. So, his road job lately had been a *sitting one.*

He sat on the ground holding a three foot spike, while two other privates alternately struck that spike with their sledge hammers. This technique, of double jacking, entailed drilling holes in rock for blasting powder. As he sat, he turned the spike a quarter turn between each hammer punch.

Bram depended on Lucent and Roy (his shoulder buddies) to make contact with the spike; not his hands or wrists. Many a sitter, such as him, had been maimed by blows on a missed target.

Bram needed his hands to make extra money for Momma.

Strike, turn, strike, turn—road building involved; drilling, blasting and clearing routes. Some say that the soldiers' telegraph lines and roads banished West Texan Comanches, more than any other military tactic.

Unfortunately, the ten-man detail would rather have been back at Fort Concho, building the chapel schoolhouse. The fort promised more comforts with a town, San Angela, across the river.

San Angela and Fort Concho were a good stopping point for Bram. When he had become a soldier there, he teamed up with another private who loved to play pranks on their company. In the army, the reward for a job well done was more hard work. So, during down time, they performed comical tomfooleries to preserve morale.

For instance, they did the *boot switcheroo* some nights. They also hid personal items. And once, Bram successfully tricked desperate young recruits into meeting non-existent ladies.

The cook let them switch blasting powder for pepper, and sugar for salt, in the mess hall.

Sometimes cook would give Bram two extra slices of bread to hide in the barracks. But Bram would tell the recruits that there were three slices. It was fun watching them frantically searching for that third fictional prize.

At Camp Charlotte, fifty miles west of the fort, the pranks were limited to tents and campfires.

No one could forget the time when Bram used grass roots to form fake spiders—to put into bedding. And once, Bram hollowed out a rotten apple; then he enclosed a live grasshopper inside. The wiggly apple became a prop in one of Bram's comic acts.

He learned as a child to style dolls from grass stems and roots, as well as string. He improvised that skill and made tiaras to put on his sleeping friends. When reveille woke the camp, hilarity ensued upon fellows finding crowns in their hair. No one felt bullied because morning was the time when everyone felt jealous of the unemployed. And it was said that *laughter is the best medicine.*

Bram was good with his hands. Hence, he never wanted the sitting job with Lucent and Roy hitting the peg.

With his skillful hands, Bram would use string and grass to make dolls to sell to men with families outside the fort. He would weave grass and roots into many other things, too.

But given a fifteen inch diameter circle of string, he could make *Jacob's ladder*, a hammock and cat whiskers. His workmates were fascinated by the many other illusions he could do with twine.

But sometimes, Bram could be shrewd with his cords and his antics.

One evening after stable and mess call, Bram set out to find a mark. He yelled, "Does anyone want to see some tricks I've been practicing?"

Roy was the only taker of the bait, though others gathered to see what Bram had in store.

"How much money do you have to bet, Roy?"

"Maybe I have four bits," he replied.

"Alright—do you mind if I borrow your wedding ring? I won't hurt it and I'll give it back shortly. I need to do a little bit of practicing on a string trick that I plan on doing at the fort. In the meantime, I'll make a bet with you. You will probably make some money off my mistakes while I rehearse," Bram went on.

Bram put up two bits saying that he could *successfully remove the ring from the middle of a looped string*, which was stretched taut between Roy's index fingers. Of course, after some crafty maneuvers, Bram removed the ring and won Roy's money. Transfixed, the company closed in on Bram and Roy near the campfire.

Lucent, in the audience, laughed at the blunder. Then the bookie in Lucent emerged at the opportunity of another trick. Men started fingering their dimes.

"I need to run through another illusion for back home. It could be a way for you to win your money back because I'm just training myself. Roy, do you want to try?"

Frustrated Roy nodded.

Glances within the group were exchanged and Lucent started taking bets.

"See my mug of cold coffee on the rock?"

"Sure," Roy responded.

"See my hat? Here, hold my hat. There's nothing odd about our military issued hat, right? So you're going to bet me two bits to do the trick, right?"

"Yes," said Roy.

"Don't you want to hear what the trick is first?"

"That's probably a good idea." Roy rolled his eyes.

"The trick is that if you place my hat over the coffee, I will never touch the hat; but will *still* drink all my coffee. Yes, I will drink that coffee from the cup without touching the hat. Go ahead and put my hat over the coffee on the rock. Do you still want to bet me, then? I bet you two bits I can drink my coffee without touching the hat."

Roy nodded.

So Bram pantomimed drinking his coffee, and then smiled big.

"That coffee was good," emphasized Bram.

Roy countered, "You didn't drink the coffee."

"Sure I did."

"No you didn't."

Roy picked up the hat. "See the coffee is still there."

"You're right." Bram said as he grabbed and drank the coffee quickly. Can I have your two bits now? I drank it without touching the hat."

Half the men groaned while the others chuckled.

At that point, Bram didn't pull any more shenanigans. He didn't want to press his luck.

In his tent that night, Bram had a strange dream. In it, a demon and angel sat—one on each of his shoulders. One looked like Lucent and the other like Roy. Lucent was telling the Aesop's fable, *The Boy and the Filberts*.

Lucent recited, "As the story goes, a greedy boy was given the opportunity to remove tasty fruit from a narrow necked pitcher. He put his hand into the pitcher and grabbed as much fruit as he could. His hand was so full of fruit that he couldn't remove his hand from the pitcher. But the boy was unwilling to release *even one* filbert. So he began to cry."

Bram remembered the story from his childhood. Nevertheless, Roy finished the story for him in the dream.

"The boy's mamma said, 'Greed leads to trouble. Do not attempt too much, at once.' And so the boy released half the filberts and was free of the confines of the pitcher," said Roy.

Bram woke at revelry. It was morning.

Bram didn't know why he'd had such a dream.

But, off to work he went, as usual.

The inspections of all of the previous day's holes revealed no unexploded duds. So Lucent, Roy and Bram went to the next blasting area while the rubble of yesterday's boom was spread into road, and made into retaining walls.

Strike, turn, strike, turn–and then a near wrist smash when Roy's hammer came down wrong. Fortunately Bram had fast reflexes. But rhythms and assurances were dampened. Bram looked up to Roy and saw anger in his face.

"Why'd you have to be so greedy?" Roy asked. "I lost more than a day's wage to you last night. And you made me the laughing stock of the camp!"

Bram got up.

"Why do tricks unless I can make my mom some money?" he asked. "Do you want me to give your dollar back?"

"No, sit down. My pride's been injured. But I'll be alright."

They continued the work till it was time to fill the holes with blasting powder and feathers.

That night, alone in his tent, Bram counted the money he was saving for his ex-slave momma to get passage to the fort.

They planned for her to be a laundress there. If they were smart and lucky, someday they would own some land near the Concho River.

But success was bittersweet for Bram. The other soldiers had family members that were ex-slaves, too. Money was precious to all the privates.

The All-Black regiment of Buffalo Soldiers would continue to make roads.

They would find their way in a privileged white country, for decades.

It would take some time.

But that is another story.

CHAPTER 2

1880 Polygamy Strain

Milo knows he will die. He is so scared of how it will all end that he is driving his three wives and ten children crazy. They live on the Lipan Flat area, near San Angela, at a time when the frontier is still quite rough.

Due to Milo's fancy, the entire family lives in a sod home, with several rooms added for comfort. The children are homeschooled, as this is the 1800s out in the wild. Mostly everyone learns through trial and error, as time goes by.

Milo says, "Time is a good teacher, but it kills all its students."

No one laughs at the joke.

Milo can't get death off of his mind. Oh, he is a good father to his offspring, and he certainly made a fine home for all fourteen in the family. He even designed the habitation so that the prevailing south summer wind would funnel through the main rooms; from the back door to the front door. The home stays cool in the summer and is strong against adversaries.

For instance, the Comanches and the buffalo make a big commotion when they come through the prairie. Becoming invisible to them is the family's strategy—so everyone in the clan hides. Then, after a while, they get tired of waiting. Fortunately Milo has acute hearing, so he can ascertain when it is safe to exit the home.

He might give the *go-ahead* to his group. But that doesn't prevent his frightened kid, Arnie, from encouraging Milo to stick his head out the door to see if it is clear.

Arnie is famous for saying, "Stay calm and don't lose your head!"

Because of that remark and others like it, Milo knows why some animals eat their young.

But his ten kids aren't the only sources of agitation in his life.

Wife One (Sue) is notorious for wanting him to babysit the young ones, even though he doesn't have any milk for them. *Babies just eat, sleep, and poop all day and night.* Wanting him to watch them during the sleeping and pooping times is not something he likes to do.

"I'm the patriarch of this family, for heaven's sake! Don't ask me to be a nurse," he says.

Milo did have to admit that the wives were excellent at gathering food for their vegetarian diet—while he babysat. But during one exceptional year, the wives could find no food. A swarm of locusts had come down upon the prairie, leaving very little crop for the family.

Wife Two (Ann) says, "Let us eat the grasshoppers, as there is nothing left to have. It is OK to eat the creatures that have eaten *our* vegetation."

Milo responds, "But I don't like eating insects. They give me indigestion. You wives need to venture further out from our land and find some roots and grain for me to eat."

Concho Folks

Wife Three (Mary) argues, "It is not our job to secure *all* of the food for this family. You are the male—you should at least hunt for adequate bugs for us, even if you refuse to eat them yourself!"

And so he did.

He wondered if the magnificent buffalo and Comanches would eat grasshoppers in the *starving-to-death* situation of that year. He still had death on his mind.

My life's a poorly written book, because in the end, I will die, he thinks, philosophically. In paranoia of his own mortality, Milo fails to remember that the Comanche and the buffalo perish too.

He tries, though. He doesn't want to be a worrier; he sincerely wants to be a better father figure. He *is* still the patriarch, but he leaves a lot to be desired.

Nonetheless, his mood remains glum; one-seventh of his life is spent on Mondays—the day of cleaning debris out of the home. *What happened to my adventurous young life?* he thinks. *I used to fight other males for the reward of a wife. I scouted for danger. Now in my older years, I still live, but it seems only for the sake of my offspring.*

"And half of fatherhood is shutting up," whispers Milo to himself, when everyone thinks he is sleeping.

No one wants to hear his morbid opinions.

He doesn't shut up when he guards the children playing outside, though. Milo reflects on the evil kidnapper of the neighborhood, "I call him 'Red' for the feathers he wears."

Red has been known to snatch up playing children as entertainment. And yes—some say he eats the children. But that would be as vicious a character as the witch in *Hansel and Gretel.* And who believes that fairy tale? The saddest thing is that when the children go missing, they remain lost for eternity.

Milo sends out **loud** warnings so that the kids get inside when Red appears out of nowhere.

And Milo does more than guard duty for the family!

There's maintenance on the home that has to be done. You see, when your roof and walls are made of dirt, there is a constant need to tamp it compactly. Water leaks easily into a sod home; don't let anyone tell you different. It seems to Milo that the tamping and repair shouldn't lie only on his shoulders—he does have three wives!

Why just a month ago, Sue complained that water was leaking onto her while she slept during a rainstorm.

"You should just fix it yourself," Milo replied. "It's on your side of the room!"

And then there are the freeloaders that took up residence in one of his rooms. Jack and his small family became houseguests when they were incapable of digging their own home. They have overstayed their welcome, for sure.

One day Jack went missing while the children were napping. Word was that he was killed by his enemies. "Around here, the number-one cause of death is **not** too many birthdays," Milo told the orphans.

"One day a stuttering guy like your dad is out in the open, and he gets killed before he can finish his sentence. That's life and death on this prairie," he continued.

Fortunately, the kids were weaned and basically able to fend for themselves—and luckily, they were vegetarians. They also tolerated the loud barking in the neighborhood, better than Milo's own family.

But if it's not the kids or guests, it's something else getting Milo down.

Milo loses sleep at night for various reasons, but one thing bothers him very much—so much, in fact, that if a neighborhood apocalypse happened, his survival plan was to *die quickly*.

You see, there in the proximity of his land for his three wives and ten children are others living in their sod homes. It is rather crowded, actually.

Property lines were never formally drawn by surveyors, so there is frequent quarreling about what land belongs to whom. No fences have ever been erected; and probably never will be. "Maybe when hell freezes over," remarks Milo.

The boundaries between homes are fluid, as erosion and plant growth take over the prairie.

Conflicts arise from simple mistakes.

Once, a room at Milo's caved in, and it was easier to build another on the other side of the home than to repair it. Milo's extension overflowed onto land that supposedly belonged to a neighbor. Gosh, sparks flew.

The amount of land per neighbor is so constrained by competition that there is a need for an ambassador within each family to serve as a peacekeeper for the colony.

The males make poor envoys, as they are too inclined to fight with another male and claim the loser's wives as his own. So females become emissaries.

I know polygamy and tight-knit neighborhoods might sound archaic, but this is how Milo's culture has always been. When they gradually moved to this spot on Lipan Flat, they knew what they were getting into.

Being so collective comes in handy when it is time for courtship and group safety. But it does require that a female from each coterie become brazen enough to venture. Milo's near-adult daughter, Bridgett, filled that vacancy this year.

When I say near-adult, I mean Bridgett is a teenager who is on the verge of courtship.

But she is also a *spy*. She must go to a possible enemy's home and greet them all (both male and female) with a kiss. After they kiss her and receive hers, they will either accept her into their territory or run her off at high speed. If she is run off, apparently that family is Milo's rival.

Sometimes Bridgett is greeted with an aggressive tussle.

Fortunately, a *friendly* visit usually occurs. Gossip is shared. Living situations are ascertained. And somewhere in the conversation, Bridgett finds out if the patriarch there is either looking for another wife—or about to die.

Upon returning from her diplomatic missions, she repeats what she has heard to the family. They evaluate the situations and make decisions.

Of course, Milo's family is visited by representatives too. Everyone wants to know each other's trade.

Some of the most pressing business is how to distribute the males.

Juvenile males (Milo calls them juvenile delinquents) must either overtake their father's patriarchy or move on to a "new-to-them" home. They must fight for a wife (or wives) and figure out what to do with mothers and aunts. So communication is vital.

A lot of decisions are made before winter arrives.

Milo is sure to tell each delegate that he has no plans for retiring. "Retirement kills more than hard work ever did," claims Milo.

"As if he really works hard," his three wives chime in chorus.

Milo has slowed in his abilities. Everyone knows he is pushing close to the end of his lifespan. But he is still no doubt, an important part of the family.

Milo's son Doug has been trying to figure out his life situation, since he is one of the "juvenile delinquents."

Doug has gone so far as to map out, in the dirt, the "dying trail" for his dad.

Doug says, "Someday, you'll take this path to a land we've never seen, and it is there that you will *pass on*. It is part of our culture to end life this way. All of us will walk the dying trail too, some day."

Milo had grown used to this kind of chatter.

Doug wasn't his first juvenile son, nor would he be his last.

"It is embarrassing to have you bring up that trail right now. I treat each day as my last, and one day I'll be right," he countered. "But don't tell me I'm going away exactly now, because I'm not!"

With that, he left the safety of the home and wandered to the head of the deer trail—the trail everyone in the colony knew to be the "dying trail." Clouds were beginning to darken overhead, as his mood got more and more somber.

Concho Folks

By comparison, Eskimo elderly walk off into the cold to freeze in their sleep—when they are a detriment to their group as a whole.

In a similar way, a severely injured colonist would not put the society in danger by remaining on the premises—hence, the "trail."

That day, Doug and his juvenile brothers were the ones to lose the war of property ownership. "War doesn't determine who is right, only who is left," muttered Milo, under his breath. "I will be left standing with my goods! No one is running me off!"

But a torrential rain began to fall on Milo. He went back to his dirty home. Hard rain was rough on the home he'd made. The lowest rooms, some as deep as three yards below ground level, would fill up fast because of this storm. Everyone would need to huddle in the midlevel rooms.

But the rain did not relent; it rained heavily for days. The large family moved to the upper-level rooms, as the halls and rooms below were captured by brown, flooding water. The ceilings were leaking from water soaking in.

The whole family tried to tap the ceiling with their *noses* to make a waterproof film—but to no avail.

The jackrabbit family shuddered in the cold with the prairie dogs. All of the other colonists were also undergoing the same catastrophe; some with their boarders of snakes, burrowing owls, and cottontails.

A verdict needed to be ready—one that only the prairie dog patriarch was qualified to make. "The cover of the river trees would be better than our being out in the open. This home is about to collapse. Red-tailed hawk will get us," Milo decided.

He and the other prairie dogs followed the "dying trail."

Little did they know that the path led to a wonderful new habitat for the surviving prairie dogs.

At the new location, there would be less competition.

And Milo could continue to ponder death with his wives and children.

CHAPTER 3

1881 The Match

"Heads, you cook supper—tails, I cook. Happy the day will be when I have a wife to cook for us," said Conrad, as he threw a nickel in the air. Aaron, Conrad's brother, rolled his eyes.

The two were gathering bison bones in Tom Green County, Texas. The buffalo had laid there to rest since their massacre in the 1870s. The prairie was dotted with the white remains that provided income for Conrad and Aaron.

They were bone collectors who loaded the relics into their ox-drawn wagons. Eventually they made their way to the new town of Abilene, Texas. From there the bones traveled by train to factories, and were converted to fertilizer, buttons, handles, and china.

With one flip of the nickel, the cook was determined. Conrad never did *best two out of three*.

"I'll cook us that rattlesnake we came upon this morning. But now, I'm going to scout out a new area of buffalo ghosts," said Aaron.

Conrad took a swig of his whiskey with the complacency of a *just-fed, homeless cat*. His own welfare and income were far more important than Aaron's eerie feelings about the near-extinct breed.

Conrad was the one who acquired the wagons for the business—but it was, ironically, Aaron who did most of the grunt work. Sometimes Conrad worked very hard; sometimes, not so much.

But they had both worked solidly that day—accumulating four and a half tons. Occasionally, the bones were so abundant in one spot that they wouldn't have to move the wagon while gathering half a ton.

Other times, of course, one of them would scout an area of decade-old kills and venture back to the grazing oxen with word of where to move next. Conrad always chose the next direction in which to go with the flip of a coin—which proved useful half of the time.

Aaron's opinion of where an ensuing pile could be found was based on studying the landscape and "thinking like a mob of scared bison."

Needless to say, many times the partners didn't agree on how to run their business.

Meanwhile, in San Angela, two young barmaids were readying for another day of selling drinks and talking-singing to men. They were at a pub located on the east edge of Veck Avenue.

The pretty sisters, Julie and Magdalene, were not ladies of the evening. In San Angela, those establishments could be found on Concho Avenue, not Veck. Their pub was managed by Miss Prissy, who had an hourglass figure, where the sand *stretched out* at the bottom. All three ladies were *looked down-upon* by the more traditional women of Fort Concho and the nearby town of Ben Ficklin. But that didn't seem to matter much to the men who sought their company.

Concho Folks

Customers were required to treat the women nicely; mistreatment could result in being banned from the pub, ostracized from the community, or even killed. Conrad was on the verge of being banned from the pub. He was raunchy sometimes.

The bar was one of the few interracial institutions in town. It catered to the Black soldiers of Fort Concho across the river, to Hispanic freighters, and to Anglos. It was a place to get news, a meal, and debate the latest ideas.

It embraced the buying and selling of goods, borrowing and lending, as well as games of a wide variety; including cards and dice. And the drinking helped create a feeling of belonging to the frontier town.

It was early afternoon at the pub, and Magdalene was wiping down the tables. Julie was fidgeting, as she anticipated beer being delivered from Ben Ficklin. She was to oversee the unloading of eight kegs. The brewery charged the pub $3.50 for each keg, and then the pub charged ten cents per mug. Julie was beside herself waiting for that week's order. She read her dime novel off and on—she wasn't much of a multitasker.

"I hate this job. I wish I could find a good man to take me away from here," shouted Julie to anyone in hearing distance. A lot of good beer-drinking men patronized the pub, including Aaron. But none of them met her high standards. Julie could be rather theatrical.

When Conrad woke the next morning, he exaggerated the hangover he felt. As usual when he imbibed too much whiskey, he regretted it the next morning. He flipped his nickel to determine if he was to drink coffee or whiskey. The flip chose coffee.

Aaron had made the coffee and was about to go looking for more cow chips to fuel the fire, for frying bacon.

"This has got to be the worst coffee you've ever made," commented Conrad, as he winced at the bitterness. "But within a month, we'll have a woman with us to keep my taste buds and stomach satisfied."

Aaron doubted that. Conrad meeting someone of his same mindset would be rare.

"You know I'm right! A frontier woman—like the ones that show up in our dime novels—she would be a great asset to our team," barked Conrad.

Aaron remarked, "I think the dime novels are exaggerated, Conrad."

Conrad shouted, "Well, we need a woman and that's that!"

The men continued to talk about politics, religion, and how to save the world. Aaron was mostly a listener since Conrad held center stage. Conrad, at the rate he was going, would have a sunburned tongue by the time they got to San Angela on Saturday. Talk is cheap.

After breakfast, they went back to work. At one pile of sun-bleached bones, a huge *eight inch* wasp nest, resided. Aaron got stung a few times but didn't make a big deal of it. Conrad got stung once and regressed to being a crybaby for half the day.

Walk, pick up—walk, load—walk, pickup—walk, load. They needed eight tons per wagon for the trip to Abilene. Time carried on without their enthusiasm.

While they were near each other at the wagon, inevitably discussions would center on the weather. It was a hot July in West Texas. In the late afternoon, storms arose with little warning. They didn't have a tent. They slept under their two wagons or out amongst the stars at night. They took cover under their slickers if it rained during the day. The bone business had begun to boom, and they were competitive. They worked rain or shine—at least Aaron did.

"You know," said Conrad, "if I get married soon, I'll probably have to buy a tent, or a covered wagon for her. Chances are she won't want to sleep in the rough, like we do."

Aaron replied, "You don't even have a girlfriend, and you're wondering about that?"

Conrad said, "I don't have a girlfriend because I'm debating about whether to get a *good* girl or a *bad* girl. *Bad* girls aren't good, but *good* girls aren't much fun. I might toss my coin on that dilemma, later."

As they made their way to San Angela, they filled their wagons to the brim. Therefore, they had some time to be alone while in transit—each on one of the wagons.

Conrad was thinking about getting the six dollars per ton of bones in Abilene.

Aaron was thinking about getting a wife. But he thought it better that she stay in San Angela, nice and safe whilst he and Conrad traveled. He dared not mention any of this to his brother, as Conrad was very opinionated and domineering.

At the pub, Miss Prissy had arranged a civilized boxing match for Saturday night. Even though she was older than God knows, she still knew how to run a bar.

It was the morning of the event, and there was much to be done by Miss Prissy, Julie, and Magdalene. Spittoons had to be dumped and cleaned. A thick stew needed to be prepared, and glassware required washing and drying.

Magdalene had an *allergy-spawned* headache but still managed to pull her weight with the chores. Julie, on the other hand, was reading her dime novel and complaining.

"My new shoes have given me six big blisters. I don't think I can work tonight," she said to Miss Prissy.

"Maybe you can tend the bar tonight. That way you won't have to do so much walking," replied Miss Prissy. "Remember to serve diluted tea to Magdalene and me if the gentlemen order us a whiskey. The tea glass should be in my left hand, so I don't get confused."

"But be sure to charge the guy for whiskey, though."

"Yes, ma'am," Julie replied. Suddenly she shouted, "Oh my goodness, my left shoe has dog poo on it! I thought I smelled something! Blisters and dog dung—this is going to be a rotten day."

Julie continued bellyaching about all kinds of drama. She mentioned that Fort Concho officers' wives *had it in for her* because they were spider-web fragile and had as many snotty attitudes as fish have bones.

"Did you hear what I said?" yelled Julie to Magdalene.

"If you must know, I'm ignoring you because I have a headache," retorted Magdalene.

"Maybe you have a headache because your halo is on too tight," snapped Julie. "You just don't get it! I'm trying to get an unmarried officer to court me, but the wives of the married officers think I'm dirt. They sully me with their high-and-mighty gossip. They whitewash themselves by blackening me," she continued. "I hate them!" She paused, and then continued, with a whimper in her voice, "But I want to be friends with them."

Just then a smelly man, whose only exercise was hiccupping, walked into the pub and ordered a drink. Miss Prissy obliged, then left the bar to check on the stew. Magdalene was still sweeping and mopping. The man then stood near Julie and read over her shoulder.

Julie was annoyed, to say the least.

"Are you girls *good* or *bad*?" asked the stranger.

"If you want to bed someone, you are in the wrong place," answered the girls simultaneously. They'd repeated that line hundreds of times.

"Oh, so you claim to be good girls, eh? Good girls are just bad girls who haven't been caught yet," he countered.

He slurped down the drink, put the glass on the bar, and then—in a blaze—went behind the bar and grabbed a full flask. The pub was being robbed of top-shelf whiskey!

He hightailed out the door and was on his way down Concho Avenue, where Conrad and Aaron were coming out of a general store.

Hastily, Conrad flipped his nickel to see who of the two was going to chase and tackle the obvious thief. The loser of the toss took that bad boy down and returned the flask to Miss Prissy, who'd been involved (belatedly) in the pursuit herself.

Concho Folks

After gawking, the rubberneckers of the town resumed their readying for another week on the frontier. There was a boxing match that night, which was like icing on the cake, for a Saturday.

Conrad and Aaron were excited about the boxing match, too. They'd already found a spot near the makeshift boxing ring made of four chairs and rope. The fight arena was outside by a lone mesquite tree next to the pub. Miss Prissy moved everything outside, because she expected a bigger crowd than her small pub could accommodate.

Conrad was enjoying a whiskey on his *straight, undiluted road to ruin*. Aaron treasured his beer from Mr. Wolter's **Ben Ficklin Brewery**. Aaron hadn't had a beer since the last time he'd visited a pub. He couldn't take a keg with him on his bone wagon.

Conrad eyed both Magdalene and Miss Prissy, who were waiting-on and singing-to the gathered customers. "Both of those waitresses look stout enough to be bone-picker wives," he said to Aaron.

Aaron wasn't paying attention to Conrad, as the fight was about to begin. Instantly bookies materialized out of nowhere and began taking bets.

Joe and his nemesis Jack were the two fighters. The spoon clanged on the pot, and the round began. The contenders danced and punched with the anger of coyotes. The people clawed their way to a better view—some stood on tiptoe.

The fight was in the third round when Joe landed multiple jabs, and Jack countered with a strong right cross. Joe was down for the count. The crowd roared. Joe was as still as a tombstone. The referee was counting... eight, nine... when Joe kicked-up and was back on his feet. Half the onlookers were delighted; the other half groaned.

Just at that moment, a shrill shriek pierced the air, and the spectators changed their priorities—smoke was pouring from a nearby barn. In a town of closely built, wooden structures, no one could ignore a fire.

Every capable person attempted to save the barn and San Angela. Aaron chose to help release the animals and save the equipment inside. Conrad had flipped a coin and was fated to join the bucket brigade near the source of the fire. Miss Prissy stayed at the pub to protect the beverages from looters.

Amazingly—Julie, and not so amazingly, Magdalene—were in the brigade. One was in front of Conrad, and the other was behind him. The buckets of water were quickly passed from person to person in a chain of human concern. Through diligence, they had the fire out relatively fast.

When the flames were extinguished, and everyone was safe, the town wondered if they should resume the boxing match. Both Joe and Jack had been in the bucket brigade, working as best friends. They were tired—depleted of adrenaline.

There would be no bare-knuckle champ that night because of the fire.

So the bookies returned the bets, and everyone celebrated having saved the barn. They shared fellowship instead of a match.

Later, Conrad and Aaron were sitting at a table with beers in hand. Conrad was smiling big—he had fallen in love with both Julie and Magdalene.

He then flipped a coin to reveal who he should pursue. When it landed, Conrad said, "This doesn't look good."

Aaron laughed.

Conrad then did something else he had never done before—he tossed the coin two more times.

CHAPTER 4

1881 The Rough One

The peculiar hitchhiker was moseying next to his limping horse on the side of the dirt road. From behind, Alphonse approached uneasily with his peddler wagon. Alphonse debated whether he wanted to pick up the barefoot guy. *Could he be trusted?*

But something about the fella made him dawdle the wagon and ask, "Want a ride?"

The frowning stranger took his time, tying his horse's reins to the wagon.

"My horse threw a shoe," said the guest, as he hoisted himself onto the seat of the dray.

The wagon resumed its journey toward San Angela. Both commuters were uncomfortably silent, as noisy sheep scattered on the prairie.

Finally Alphonse asked, "Where are you headed?"

"Knickerbocker," scratched the passenger.

"Well that's on my way. I think we just follow Dove Creek downstream, and we'll be there before you know it," Alphonse answered.

More silence ensued. *Is this hitchhiker just uncommunicative, or is he scheming a theft?* Alphonse thought.

"Say—have you had any trouble getting rides?" Alphonse broke the quiet.

"Yes," was the grunted response.

"What's your name, if you don't mind my asking?" Alphonse queried.

"Ned Land," the guy replied, as curtly as possible.

Alphonse was content, since he now had a name for the face.

"How did you know that I wasn't going to rob you when I picked you up, Ned?" he continued.

Ned smirked and said, "Guys like us know when we can clobber a man or not. You don't look that tough to beat."

The driver countered, "Well, I'm just a pots and pans salesman. I'm low on cash since most people barter for my wares. But I ain't gonna mess with the likes of you."

A hush occurred while they snaked their way along the creek on the dusty road.

Finally, out of courtesy, Alphonse asked, "What kind of work do you do?"

Ned's nostrils flared as he mouthed deliberately, "That's none of your business!"

Shaking his head, Alphonse assumed he'd have no more conversation with his new acquaintance.

But much later, for no reason at all, Ned snapped, "If you must know, I'm a spotter for Jimbo. When he's struggling with wrestling rough individuals, I take over. My friends and I are also scouters in the wild."

After a moment, "So, you're in some kind of gang, like Buffalo Bill's?" asked the driver.

"We ain't no dime novel riffraff," replied the offended passenger.

"Well, why are you stopping in Knickerbocker? Shouldn't you and your band be going further, to San Angela, to clean up that town?" Alphonse probed.

"Our business is miles *up*stream. We don't go where there's too much howling and festive drunkards. We hate card sharks and men sulking at bars. Dove Creek is our lair."

Alphonse was impressed with the discourse.

"Jimbo's the leader of our group. And we're not elegant beings! We've broken from civilization for reasons I will not disclose. And we do not obey the rules," Ned shouted.

"OK, don't get lathered up," criticized Alphonse.

"We're misunderstood. Every day we tour Dove Creek on our raft. The three of us look for settlers having trouble with bad individuals," he bragged.

He continued, "Why, I killed my first river monster two years ago. It was a five-foot-long water moccasin. It had been bothering Miss Belle. So for an hour, the beast and I wrestled till it succumbed. Then last year, a forty-five-pound snapping turtle was causing problems for the Shafer family. Jimbo and I grappled together on that giant. His shell was half a yard wide! He became a fine turtle soup."

Alphonse thought about Ned's responses for a twinkling of time. He didn't want to belittle Ned, but he had to ask, "So, your gang protects settlers from river monstrosities?"

Ned replied, "It's not that simple! We don't carry firearms! Have you ever brawled with an alligator gar that is eight feet long and weighs 250 pounds?"

Ned barked, "Well, I have!"

"But why did you manhandle a gar when you could have just speared it?" the peddler inquired.

"Our group didn't have a harpoon when the Lopez family was destitute. We had to make do with the situation at hand."

With raised eyebrows, the trader looked ahead, feeling cantankerous about his odd traveler. After taking a deep breath, he probed, "What else have you killed with your bare hands?"

"Well for fun, the crew and I sometimes noodle catfish out of their egg hole. Jimbo wraps a rag around his arm when we've found the tunneled daddy-fish. Then he sticks his arm into the hollow and wriggles his fingers. Pierre and I are on both sides of Jimbo, in case the giant takes him down."

"Well, I take that back. Half the time, Pierre isn't in the water with us. He's writing a dime novel about it. At any rate, I help Jimbo bring the catfish to shore. Those seventy-pounders sure make for good eating."

Though Alphonse could go on listening to this routine for hours, he could see the lantern lights of Ned's town up a little ways.

"What's your horse's name?" asked Alphonse during their final moments together.

"Why, he's Nemo, of course."

That figures, thought the merchant.

Before Ned could brag any further about wrestling twenty-five-pound soft-shelled turtles or twelve-pound largemouth bass, Alphonse asked which direction he should take to get to Ned's nighttime terminus.

"Right up the road at that wooden shack. See the man holding a book and a lantern?" he whispered.

They made their way there.

Then they stopped at the hut. Ned got down, untied Nemo from the wagon, and led him to the barn.

When Ned was out of earshot, Alphonse said to the man, "I see that Ned has a good place to rest up for tomorrow's exploits."

Mr. Land patted the book, "I was reading *Twenty Thousand Leagues Under the Sea* when Ned was born, eleven years ago."

"We've read the book countless times since then."

"So, his daily recollections of upstream events are always bizarre."

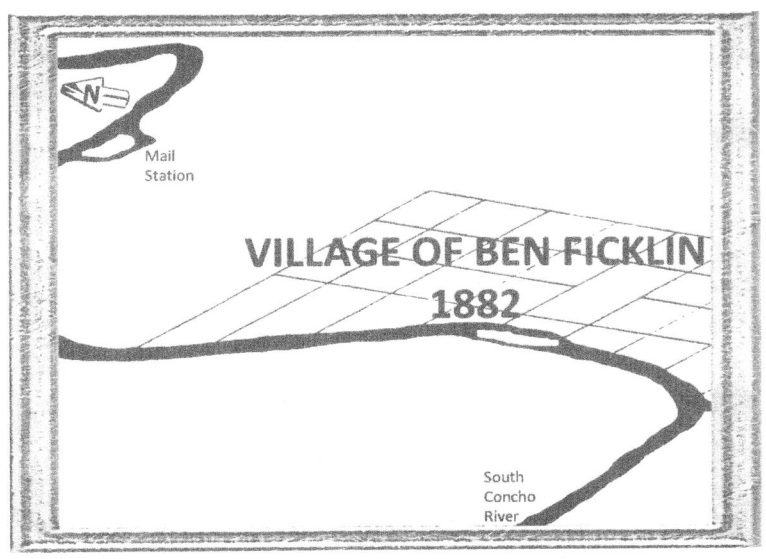

Map labels:
- Mail Station
- VILLAGE OF BEN FICKLIN 1882
- South Concho River

CHAPTER 5

1882 Ben Ficklin...
Two Weeks Before

L ately, Hugo has been a lightning rod for criticism. His wife, Sadie, wanted him to make choices that exhausted him. Being pampered, she never really knew what it took to be a well-rounded businessperson living in the small town of Ben Ficklin. But in all fairness, she had her moods, and he had his—so, they were equal in many respects.

As Hugo left their home on the courthouse square the morning of August 9, 1882, he grabbed an umbrella for the likelihood of rain. He left Sadie complaining about breakfast being cold. Her maid was incompetent, she thought, because the cook stove had little dry wood.

But he, escaping into the day, was thankful that the rain had relented for a while. There had been so much moisture for a week, mud was everywhere. Little did he know that it was the beginning of a rare monsoon season in the Concho Valley.

Fortunately, the wooden sidewalks prevented him from muddying up to his knees. The same footways became the playpen of children whose parents needed to get them out of their hair.

Some girls were playing hopscotch. As Hugo walked around and through them, he gave each of them a morsel of candy he'd pocketed before leaving the house. Sometimes it was his custom to tickle the fancy of the rascals. Their parents didn't mind.

The town was only a few hundred persons big, and everyone knew each other.

There were the visitors, of course, but overall you could trust the strangers as well.

Hugo made his way to the new courthouse, tipping his hat to the ladies and winking at their babies. He gave up his place in line for an older gentleman and complimented the clerk for his efficiency. After taking care of business at the courthouse, he wandered down to the hotel for a cup of coffee.

There, he gave up his table in the crowded dining area for a traveling family of four. A fussy youngster couldn't be pacified during the meal, so Hugo offered to tell the story of *The Prince and the Pauper* by Mark Twain.

The book, which he'd bought the previous year, was kept in his jacket pocket for such a situation. Today, the whole dining area listened to him as he wowed the audience with the drama.

Hugo left the hotel dining area feeling softness in his heart. The diners were satisfied physically with the food and spiritually with the story. The tale had alleviated the dreariness of so many consecutive rainy days.

Next, when he went into his general store, he smiled at his customers. The rest of his day was spent helping others who genuinely appreciated him.

As evening drew near, he prepared for supper with his wife. He'd had a good day. He wondered what kind of trouble his wife had provided the community.

Concho Folks

Sadie was waiting for him in a darkened dining room. Supper was cold—again, it had been difficult to find any dry wood. But Hugo sat down in a cheerful mood and awaited the onslaught of vile comments from a bitter woman.

"First, I readied for the day by making the cook iron my favorite dress—you know, the one with the yellow daisies," she said. "It took a good two hours for her to starch and press it, but I do declare that I looked more beautiful in it, than any of the other ladies at the Whist Card Club."

"While playing cards, I started a tedious rumor about Eloisa. She will no longer vie for partnering with Sue at the games."

"Sue and I will be allies to the end of time."

"Kay told me a secret, which I have no intention of keeping. I'll somehow spread the secret anonymously, and she will be so embarrassed when the whole town finds out."

"I wrote a nasty letter of complaint to our county commissioner. I want something done about all the children playing on the sidewalks. They shouldn't be underfoot, and their laughter is horrendous. We had a very difficult time strategizing and making tricks with all the commotion outside. And shouldn't school start soon?"

"After cards, we went to the hotel café for a hot lunch and nearly tripped over some children acting out the pitiful story of *The Prince and the Pauper*. Really, you'd have thought they were on a stage, the way they were quoting lines and being silly—hideous, in my mind.

"And you know what I got served for a meal? A cold egg sandwich on day-old bread, that's what. Can you imagine that? I just wanted to scream. And so I did."

"After the screaming, the girls and I took a day trip to San Angela to see the wives of the fort's officers. We brought up and gossiped about the year-old court-martial of Henry O. Flipper. Then we cussed and discussed Fort Concho's Buffalo soldiers being at Fort Davis—where they belong.

"Having Fort Concho entirely Anglo made us all giggle with pleasure."

"And then I returned home."

"I'm tired. My dress is muddy and disgusting. I just want to scream."

She made her way to the bedroom trifold screen. As she undressed, she began to cry.

"I'm so tired, I just want to go to bed," she finished.

Hugo laughed quietly, and then, on an impulse of goodwill, decided to reveal his day.

He retraced his encounters.

Upon completion, he said, "And I'm not at all tired."

"And if it is of any consolation to you, dear Sadie, tomorrow I will be the *bad one*. I will spread rumors. I will also disclose secrets, make false accusations, and have a bad disposition," he continued.

"Thank goodness, Hugo," she sighed.

Then they went to bed.

Two weeks later, a flood demolished most of the town of Ben Ficklin.

Hugo and Sadie survived, though their house and store didn't.

Immediately thereafter, they relocated to San Angela and dutifully resumed their alternating days of mischief.

Hugo and Sadie oscillated behaviors.

They played—nicely sometimes—but continued gossip-mongering and *general meanness,* to keep everyone puzzled.

CHAPTER 6

1882 Pillow Emotions

Setting: The Concho Valley, Texas, from the 1860s to the 1930s

Sophia was a toddler when she acquired a pillow from her mother. Little did she know that the pillow had the ability to absorb its owner's emotions. This was a handy feature when Sophia was sad; it was as if crying into the pillow resolved all her problems.

The pillow was named "Lazarus" after a pillow fight had erupted among the cousins. Mama had to bring the pillow *back to life* by restuffing it with feathers and cotton. Maintaining that pillow would be a lifelong endeavor as Sophia matured.

But could a pillow detect sentiments? As a young girl, she would unknowingly make the pillow happy by resting her doll beside it. And the pillow felt privileged to have the tooth fairy replace Sophia's teeth with coins. Sophia evoked happiness in the little family, and the pillow responded in kind.

The small family lived at Ben Ficklin, an aspiring town in the Concho Valley. Sophia's father worked for the stage company nearby. She grew up in the fine community.

But in 1882, when Sophia was fifteen, a terrible flood wiped out the town—taking her mother and father as victims. The devastation was immense, but Sophia and Lazarus somehow survived.

She and other surviving, teenaged orphans were grouped together and moved to higher ground in San Angela. They scraped together a living there, with construction. San Angela had become a growing county seat and Ben Ficklin was not going to be rebuilt.

When autumn arrived, her group of teenagers gathered pecans at Miles Grove and shelled them for living expenses. Lazarus had lots of passions during this thrifty phase of Sophia's life. He also became stained—due to pecan-oiled fingertips—bloodied from shelling so many nuts.

In 1888 the railroad was brought to the growing city, and Sophia found the love of her life. Roger was a train employee and the sparkle in Sophia's eyes.

After marrying Roger, she spruced up Lazarus by replacing the dingy covering and washing the filling to newness. Sophia and Roger were very happy and financially well off. But because of this splendor, Lazarus became a minor piece of bedding in the new house on Abe Street. Things were going so well that Sophia sometimes forgot about her parents' tragic deaths and her difficult time as an orphan.

Lazarus was elated when Roger found out about her pregnancy. The couple shed so many tears of joy on Lazarus.

But as fate would have it, as suddenly as she had become happy with Roger in her life, Sophia was devastated when Roger was killed in a railroad accident. Losing three loved ones in a span of six years was almost more than she could bear. Her friend Kate helped console her, but ultimately *time* would have to heal her wounds.

Lazarus was put into a wooden chest, and the house was darkened as the pregnancy progressed.

In the long run, it was God's Word that helped her to see that raising the baby was the only thing she could do presently. She would have to be strong for the infant.

When Cynthia was born, Sophia's demeanor swiftly changed for the better. Light was allowed in the house, Lazarus was resurrected from the chest, and almost all was right with the world. Lazarus held the esteemed pleasure of being on the sofa with Sophia and Cynthia.

While Cynthia was growing up, Sophia volunteered in her community, later called San Angelo.

Lazarus had to be mended multiple times as the years wore on. Sophia found that using lamb's wool as stuffing was just as good as feathers and cotton.

Time went on for Sophia, Lazarus, and Cynthia.

In 1936, when Sophia was sixty-nine years old, another flood affected her.

When the flash flood warnings were announced, she grabbed Lazarus and other sentimental belongings and got to higher ground—at Cynthia's house on Eighth Street.

All of Sophia's loved ones were safe inside Cynthia's meager home. Though she was frustrated by the ruination of her house on Abe Street, she couldn't help but count her blessings.

Sophia had endured many struggles in her life, but her faith in God and her supportive friends, (Lazarus included), got her through them all.

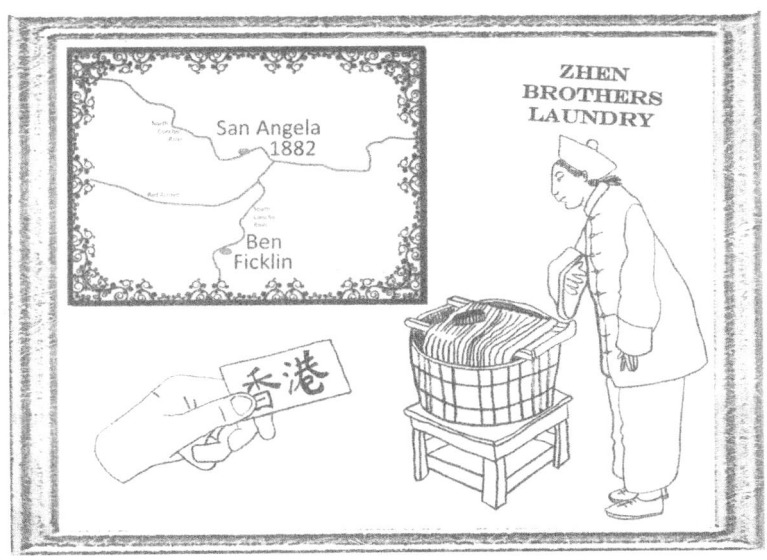

CHAPTER 7

1883 Bundle of Sticks

A ugust 8, 1883
San Angela, Texas

Dearest Mother and Father,

It is with great regret that I send you news about your son, Yong, losing a thumb on his left hand. It was no accident, I assure you. And the evil man involved *has no*t and *will not* be punished.

But I have other news, some good and some bad, to share with you.

A flood last year erased the town of Ben Ficklin, so the perfect opportunity to arrange a laundry establishment in San Angela, Texas, arose. We have been set up for business for five months now, and our routine is set. My three brothers and I work hard to send you money, as we know you really need it.

By the way, how are my friends there in Shandong? I know most of them are married, with wonderful husbands. I, of course, have no boyfriend here. My brothers make sure of that—but I'm optimistic that my coming to the USA was not a mistake. I will forever miss my deceased twin brother and you too. I wish that beast that kicked him was dead!

Our laundry is called the "Zhen Brothers Laundry," and, as far as almost everyone knows, I still pose as a male here. I couldn't help but give hints to my seamstress friends, Maggie and Laura, that I'm feminine. I told them how a US hiring agent approached Father about letting his four sons (my twin included) travel to San Francisco. They could escape the crises of China and send money home to us.

But then a week before they were to leave us, Jang was killed by that beast. I told Maggie that it was in my best interest to pose as Jang, go to the USA, and make a new life for myself. It has been incredibly hard work, but I'm hoping the money I send to you relieves you.

Let me describe my two friends, Maggie and Laura. I met them when they actually approached me. They said that if there was too much mending to be done, that they being seamstresses, could help. They could aid us when we are *too* busy, and if they're *not too* busy.

That is, in fact, how they became friends with each other. They both would go to the Nimitz Hotel and other places, such as the stage station—to offer sewing and mending services to the fine ladies. They were competing against each other and were enemies. That is, until one became too stressed by an order, while the other had no work at all. So they teamed up together. They want to band up with me, too—but I have to go behind my brothers' backs to subcontract some extreme sewing projects to them. I'm always so busy that I think I'll go crazy sometimes. I don't mind paying them a fair price, occasionally, so that I don't have to work an eighteen-hour day.

Concho Folks

I'm learning English! I'm better at it than my brothers. I have to translate for them all the time. This is a burden to me. But being the youngest, they say I pick up English faster than them. Sometimes Maggie and Laura have been in the shop when an order comes in *or* is leaving. They help me with my communication.

For instance, I have to explain to the customer what I'm writing on their pickup ticket. They don't like the Chinese characters. Some of them think I am writing a bad word on the ticket. Many times Laura has interceded, and everyone would leave in peace.

Some people don't keep up with their pickup ticket! They may think that the Chinese characters are just decorations, I guess.

A man named Alejo did just that. He discarded his ticket. When he wanted to pick up his clothing, I showed him the ledger and the paper packages of clean clothes and asked him if he knew which was his. He got very angry with me.

I'm not sure what all he said, but it felt like he was threatening our very lives over his lost piece of paper. Maggie came into the store and we resolved the crisis—but not before he threw my abacus on the floor, scattering beads throughout the shop.

One time when Yong was not chopping wood for the washing water, someone robbed our clotheslines of drying garments. We did not get much sympathy from the sheriff when we reported the theft. He said that this was what happened when we don't guard our laundry.

We took a financial loss when that occurred, as there had been some pretty lady dresses on the line at the time of the theft.

Another setback involves fire insurance. We are in a wooden building and are expected to contribute to the block's fire-protection fund. This is because our shops are almost all connected and certainly all wooden. If Yong was to mismanage our woodstove fire, then everyone's place on the block would almost certainly burn, too. What is unfair though, is the amount we are to pay. It is not equitable to the Anglos' bills. We pay almost twice that of the neighboring businesses.

Maggie says, "Just pay the extra money and let it be." But she's not the one who works sixteen hours a day! There's cutting wood, hauling water from the river, tending the fire, and buying the soap, starch, and other supplies. There's the actual washing, rinsing, wringing, drying, ironing, and packaging to do. There's working with the customers. Then, of course, there's the mending (a chore my brothers won't do).

One time we did not pay the money on time. Yong was at the river with our rented mule and the water-barrel cart. As he was bucketing water into the barrel, Alejo came up to him from behind and wrestled him into the water. He tried to drown him!

Fortunately, Yong is like one of the brothers in the story called *"Ten Chinese Brothers"* that you have fondly told us. Yong held his breath so well that Alejo got tired of the whole thing, shouted something and then left. (Yong does have a talent for holding his breath for a very long time—great lungs!)

But Yong was not to be so lucky another time, as he does not have the talent of a steel neck or thumb, as in the story of the brothers. A masked man, who we are nearly certain, was Alejo, snuck up on Yong while he was sawing wood to fit into our stove. (Yong really is a terrific worker.)

Anyway, he spoke to Yong in some gibberish and roughed him up a bit. When Yong remained noncompliant, a second masked man entered the drama. Yong could understand some of what the second thug was saying, and it had to do with Chinese in general. They just don't like us "coolies."

Anyway, they managed to take the ax and cut his left thumb off as if it were nothing! Yong's left hand now is no better than a dog's paw! It healed, as I sewed it shut after washing it with whiskey. Brother Fu is taking on the chopping and water hauling for our business now in Yong's stead.

You would think that the mean people would eventually get bored of harassing us. Maggie says to comply and pay the extra money. Laura says it's extortion and is outrageous. But what are our options? Laura says that we could do laundry in a more hospitable town. "You should move," she says, "to protect yourselves."

Maggie has more hope for the situation; she says that they will eventually come to accept us. It is so confusing. We work harder than the Anglos. We stay sober. We offer services that they need! What to do, what to do?

And Mother, did I mention that I really miss my true love in China? I am crying as I write this because I know Quing married Li Jie. My heart breaks when I think of them.

I truly regret what I have to tell you next, my dear parents. I will start by saying that I am shaken, but alright.

There was an incident that was supposed to happen to another brother, I think, but because we all dress alike, and everyone thinks I'm a man, I turned out to be the unlucky one. It happened a week ago.

I was walking back to the laundry from the river late one stormy evening. Four men on horses came upon me during my hurried steps. Most of the town was readying for sleep. I consider that part of the day to be my personal quiet time when I can worship. How they knew I was down at the river, I have no idea. Maybe they'd been stalking me and knew my pattern of behavior.

But for whatever reason, one of them grabbed me—pinned me to him and put his other hand over my mouth. I was so surprised and confused. I thought, *Am I going to lose a thumb, too?*

What happened to me was something no one dreams of happening. I was taken to a secluded area in a field surrounded by scrubby trees. My screams reached no ears. I was then gagged and told I'd be dismembered—as an example to any Chinaman who didn't comply with their demands. I didn't really understand what they were saying, but I understood their tone. I also understood that I was doomed.

They tied four ropes to my hands and feet. Then they stretched the long ropes north, south, east, and west. They were in the process of tying the ropes to their saddle horns when a bolt of lightning struck nearby. The thunder came next. The lightning made the hairs on my neck stand upright. One of the men began to have second thoughts about pulling my limbs from my torso. He said he had religion, and he knew a sign from God when he saw one.

During this time I was still stretched somewhat, but not to the point of real pain. The men discussed the situation, and I was freed after a stern lecture on how useless I am. I fled.

So you see, dear parents, I was not hurt. Maggie and Laura were so upset when I told them what happened. Laura said I was lucky that they didn't realize I was a woman, or they would have raped me, as well.

Maggie told me a story from *Aesop's Fables*. It was about sticks. She said that it is easy to break a stick by itself, but it is difficult (if not impossible) to break sticks when they are in a bundle. She said she had heard that more Chinese persons were coming into town to start laundries and restaurants. "You can stop the bullying as a unified group," she said.

At first I cringed. Competition would be hazardous to our livelihood. How can we send money to China if we don't have enough customers. But then Maggie and Laura explained that with San Angela being the new county seat, it was becoming a very prosperous place.

So Mother, your sons and I are between phases of cultural development here. Hopefully, we will form our own little China town in San Angela. Maybe I'll find a man to replace my love, Quing. Maybe I will no longer have to pose as a man to get by in this society. Maybe people will change.

I end this letter asking for your thoughts for us. We are afraid, but not for much longer.

Your loving daughter,
Jin Zhen

CHAPTER 8

1884 As Good As It Gets

"I know you can hear me. There's no need to pout," Carla said upon entering their bedroom. "I merely went to the *San Angelo Standard Times* to advertise my elixir for aches and pains. Then I picked up my delivery of brown-glass bottles and labels," she continued.

It was a hot day in July of 1884. She hated that George was sulking because she'd left without his permission earlier.

And George was not well.

Yesterday, she'd found him wandering around the property, as if looking for shade.

She lured him back inside and gave him water. Carla was beginning to think that George was losing his mind. Why else would he feel the need to escape their hut near the Concho River? *It is too hot to hunt,* she thought.

And he was in no condition to do much of anything; a feral cat in the neighborhood had given him cat-scratch-fever two days prior.

Certainly, her elixir could fix George's infection. If only she could convince him to drink it.

They say that you can lead a horse to water, but you can't make him drink.

Ah, but George was not a horse. He was her live-in friend of a few months.

"My dear, you know I seldom make errors, and even if I had made a mistake, there is no reason for you to slump. I know you will be well soon and fit enough to dominate your world," she bellowed at the bedroom's entrance.

She left the doorway to toil with her still. Her elixir was a secret recipe, handed down to her by her father. It required patient tending, as the temperature of the fire must be very accurate. She'd been collecting wood for a similar fire, months prior, when she happened to meet George.

Since then, they had been living together.

George was a great bedroom companion.

Her old dog, Juju thought otherwise. He had a habit of staring at George for long periods of time. This probably frustrated George. It is common for males to vie for a female's attention, and George and Juju were no exception.

Carla made herself a cup of tea and read last Saturday's newspaper. Her idea to have an advertisement for her elixir had been spur of the moment this morning. And her decision to leave the hut without so much as a word to George was, perhaps, unconventional in her mind.

As she rested on her chair, her aching feet began to throb.

"You know, I have to make this elixir for our livelihood. I know my craft takes a lot of my time away from you—what with the distilling, bottling, and labeling," she shouted to the bedroom, as she began to inscribe labels at the little table.

Still no reply from George. *Is he asleep?* She wondered, as she continued carefully writing on the labels.

"Someday I'm going to be so successful that I will have the labels printed at the newspaper office," she said, as she began to mix water with powdered glue for the labels.

Still no reply from George—

Juju was napping on the floor beneath George. There was no attachment between the two males; it might even be that George and Juju hated each other. Carla wasn't certain.

Later, Carla was gathering the alcohol for her elixir. She had multiple jars of steeped herbs and seeds on the shelf, as her recipe dictated. It came time to strain the concoctions and mix the liquids in the correct proportions with the booze.

"You know, I might have made a slight error today. And I mean a very slight fault by not telling you about my excursion this morning. But seriously, this pouting is boring me silly."

She drank a spoonful of the elixir in her capacity as quality control.

"George, this batch seems to be my best. I feel like I can advertise it as healing warts and pink eye—as well as aches and pains."

George was still silent. This frustrated Carla. *How can I get him to quit being mad at me?* She wondered.

"Well, I'm taking these filled bottles to the general store. I will be back shortly," she eventually said, as she hoisted the wooden box of medicine on her hip. She sipped another spoonful of her potion from the bowl on the table. "Yes, this is my best batch ever," she concluded.

"Now Juju, stay out of the solution while I'm gone," she said. With that, she departed again.

When she left, Juju got up and went to the table to inspect the elixir. Upon licking some of it, he resumed his position on the dirt floor under George.

Juju thought, *It is unlikely that George will ever forgive Carla for her blunder.*

When Carla returned with some food from the store, she noticed that the table had been disturbed.

"Oh yes, you did it, George! You finally had some elixir. Did it boost your spirits and help your infection? I knew you'd come around to seeing that I'm just a woman who can make slip-ups. I promise I will always let you know when and where I go."

Carla put away the flour, sugar, and bacon for which she'd bartered. Then she worked again with her still.

Eventually, she left word with the fellas that she was going to go to the mill to get more corn for her mash. Juju got up and walked her to the door.

"You are such a good boy, Juju." She petted him.

"George, I love you and am sorry I made you so angry today," she yelled. Then she left.

The lizard, George, was still motionless in his box habitat in the bedroom; he hadn't moved a speck since morning.

It seems Carla no longer had two animals to love. Because when she had left early that morning, Juju and George fought for Carla.

And Juju won.

Satisfied, Juju carried dead George back to the woodpile.

Carla will recover, he thought.

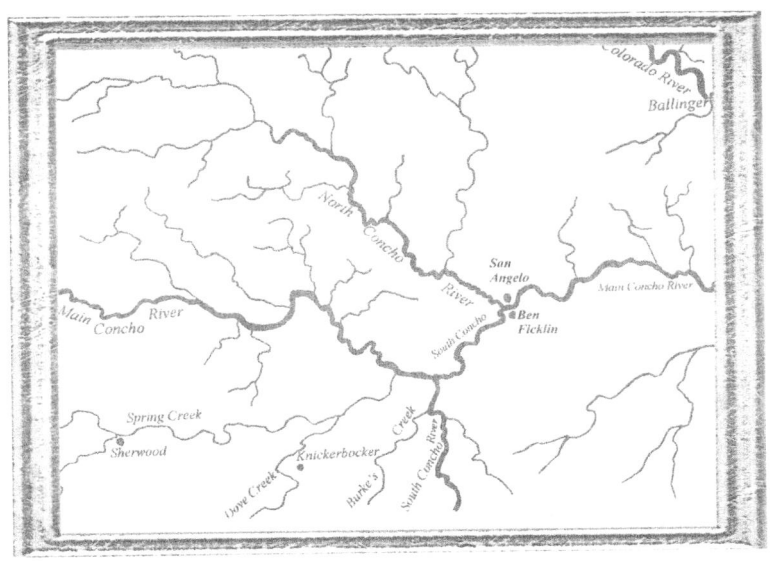

CHAPTER 9

1884 Shy

"He said he hated my mother, he hated my father, and he hated me. Then I was falling out of the canoe," Rosheen wailed, as I helped her out of Dove Creek.

I had been traveling with my horse, Sneed, when I heard the deafening screams of a woman in distress. So as I was pulling her muddied ego out of the river, I couldn't help but wonder what I'd gotten myself into.

Sneed and I were on our way to go to work at the *Angelo Journal Newspaper* on Oakes Street. I'd been in correspondence with Mr. Acker there, while I lived in Fredericksburg. West Texas called out to me and my rigorous, insanely accurate ways. Errors in my hometown paper were few and far between because of my rigidity. I had promised Mr. Acker to be the same for him.

In case you wondered, my name is Shiloh, and I was born nineteen years ago—the year that Abe Lincoln was killed. My parents left to see the Lord two years ago, and I've been on my own ever since. I wear my hair up in a flattering style and almost always wear black clothing, especially when I'm typesetting. I'm shy, and I have a secret about myself that I am unwilling to share with others. So I keep to myself to prevent the public from finding out—I don't want their sympathy.

"Sneed, be good while I help her pack," I said, as I brought him a bucket of water.

Rosheen had been good company in my wagon. We were about to pack up her belongings at her cabin—and head on, so she could catch a stagecoach. She would go back to her parents in Illinois to escape her belittling spouse, she said. I helped her pack her two gray bags with her clothing. I noted that we wore about the same size—she also had a hefty waist and small breasts. One might say that we were both kind of *linear*.

Nevertheless, we got her clothes and were working on kitchen items that she could sell—to get train fare at Fort Worth. Anything of value was captured quickly and boxed in a large crate in the back of my wagon. She was so nervous that her husband would find her leaving and prevent it. She'd thought of this day hundreds of times, and it was finally here.

"I'm so lucky you came along when you did," remarked Rosheen.

"I can't imagine living with a man like yours for as long as you did. Maybe he didn't put his hands on you to smack you around, but he was still controlling, blatant, and disrespectful," I said.

"I would always think that, in the future, he would be better, you know?" Rosheen finished packing the last of her things. "Oh, I almost forgot—I'd hate for him to find this under the mattress someday."

She'd darted to the bed.

She pulled out an obscure cardboard box with a womb veil in it. "He shames me for being infertile, because we haven't had any children. I owe my lack of being a mom to this handy device that I mail ordered soon after realizing he is so arrogant."

"Why'd you stay with him so long? Didn't you realize he was deflating you? I suspect he alluded that he is perfect, and you aren't. I've seen others like him. Also, I bet he is really handsome," I alleged, as Sneed responded to my reins.

Rosheen looked back longingly to the cabin behind us and remarked, "Voices told me to leave, but it was just too hard until you came along."

After a while, we no longer thought that every noise nearby was her husband hunting us down. So at some point, I stopped the wagon and found a private place for Rosheen to get out of her wet clothing. We were on the banks of the Concho, edging closer to the stagecoach station, where the stage would take her to Fort Worth.

While she was changing, I remembered that my uncle was a lot like her husband. Once before my own puberty, I was at his house whittling wood in the middle of the day. He said to me that he was a nothing and yet *he* was all that he could think about. Then he switched gears and actually seemed interested in me—saying, "But I will now concentrate on you."

My eyes brightened, but without further ado, he asked me if I thought *he* was a good man. Before I could respond, he became arrogant about his accomplishments. It turns out that most of *his* good deeds were actually completed by my aunt. This was his typical behavior.

I mentioned this memory to Rosheen and observed the expression on her face. She was predictably lost in thought. There were some nods and an "ah-ha" as she re-evaluated her own marriage.

Rosheen described, "I'll never forget what happened when we were in the canoe. I was telling him how I missed my family. Before I knew what was happening, he was trying to manipulate me into never seeing them again. He said he'd burn all of their letters to me, unopened. He was so sneaky when he purposely rocked the boat so I would fall into the creek. To sulk, he probably went to his pathetic *secret* place, where he keeps his stash of booze. And all because I said I would divorce him someday."

What could I say to her? I felt such sympathy, but I didn't understand why she seemed to take responsibility for him being pathetic towards her. After other discussions during the ride, I found out that she is also superstitious. How do you reason with a person who thinks she was doomed to have bad luck—because she broke a mirror three years ago?

"God bless her," I remarked to Sneed, as I was feeding him that evening.

We settled for the night near Ben Ficklin Quarry (only we didn't know it at the time). I slept under the wagon, as I usually do. She slept in a makeshift tent fashioned with my slicker. The next morning arrived with the sound of a very loud blast. The explosion and tumbling of rocks shook the ground. She feared that the noise had something to do with her husband. I thought, *All my aspirations of being an editor someday have been extinguished like a candle.*

After realizing that we weren't going to die, we investigated our camp's perimeter and realized where we were. I have to say that a quarry is a neat place to be if you love rocks. The crew was at work, moving boulders and cutting stones to manageable sizes. Some craftsmen, as artistically as a woodpecker, were making dimensional blocks for the Tom Green County Courthouse.

We stayed for a bit, since the stage in Angelo would probably leave that afternoon; and our only concern was being followed by her angry husband. During the crew's morning break, Rosheen (upon my advice) tried to sell some of her wares for the money she would need for passage between San Angelo and Chicago.

The coffeepot sold, as did several items from the kitchen. The men had little use for her girlish things, as they were away from their wives for the duration of the building of the courthouse.

One man really was squeamish about the womb veil she had laid on her blanket with her jewelry. None of the men wanted to ask what it was, but in their hearts, they had their guesses.

After we had sold all that we could in the limestone camp, we got Sneed ready for the last little stretch of the ride to Angelo. The wagon, though being a little bit lighter, still moved slowly on the much frequented road. There was a part of me that wanted to scout for a less rutted road paralleling the one we were on. But I just didn't want to leave Rosheen alone because of the possibility of *you-know-who* catching up with us.

Eventually, we reluctantly parked by the river for Sneed's water break. Rosheen and I went separate ways in the bushes. My break took longer than hers, as I had taken my toiletry kit with me.

Getting into town was by no means easy, but we made it. Rosheen's *soon-to-be* ex-husband was nowhere to be seen, thankfully. I parked Sneed and the wagon in front of the Nimitz Hotel, where we hoped to sell her goods to its guests. I had no idea that, in a sizeable crate, in my wagon box was a miniature harp. When she opened her crate, there were tears in her eyes that, to me, meant that the harp was a family heirloom. She lifted the harp out carefully and began to play an Irish tune. This drew a sizeable crowd to the wagon, and I knew that people would offer, for her wares, enough money for her trip.

Since she had everyone's attention with the harp, she laid out almost all of her belongings (thankfully, not her womb veil) in the back of my wagon. She explained her desire to go to Chicago and asked if anyone in the small crowd knew how much money she would need to get there safely. Someone replied, and I'm sure her heart sank as the quarry deposit was not near enough money. She didn't want to part with her father's pocket watch or the harp, but she was desperate.

A few of the ladies in the crowd bought hat pins and costume jewelry. But a big purchase was necessary to make the goal. Two men wanted the harp, so an impromptu auction ensued. Because she was brokenhearted, I started the bid at a reasonable amount. Then the men bid openly against one another.

At some point, when it seemed that the trip fund to Chicago would be complete, the saloon keeper next door came out. He mentioned that neither of the two twits had that much money on them; for if they did, the money should go toward their bar tabs at his establishment.

Someone yelled, "Let's bid on the harp again!"

It was with reluctance that I started the bidding again. And this time the bidding was with new, respectable persons who had come out of the hotel because of the previous loud bidding. The harp sold, and Rosheen was to be on the stagecoach shortly.

"Goodbye, sweet friend! Shiloh, I don't know what I would have done without you." She said this to me as if we'd known each other for years, instead of a day. We had done a lot of talking on our way to San Angelo.

"I know we'll see each other in another time, Rosheen," I said, as my ward was entering the stagecoach.

As I was holding the two gray bags with her dresses in them, she quietly said, "I want you to have one of the bags, to show my appreciation for your efforts and advice. Take either the green one or the red one, your choice."

They both looked gray to me, so I chose one for myself, and the driver lifted her other bag to the top of the coach. He tied it down with the other passengers' bags.

"Goodbye, Rosheen."

"Goodbye, Shiloh."

My adventures with Rosheen had started and ended within twenty-four hours. She, among others, never suspected anything about me.

I will start typesetting at the newspaper tomorrow as a woman with a manly figure. I will take my toiletry kit and shave my face twice a day in the outhouse behind Oakes.

I will remain forever grateful that I didn't get the gray luggage with a *useless-to-me* womb veil in it.

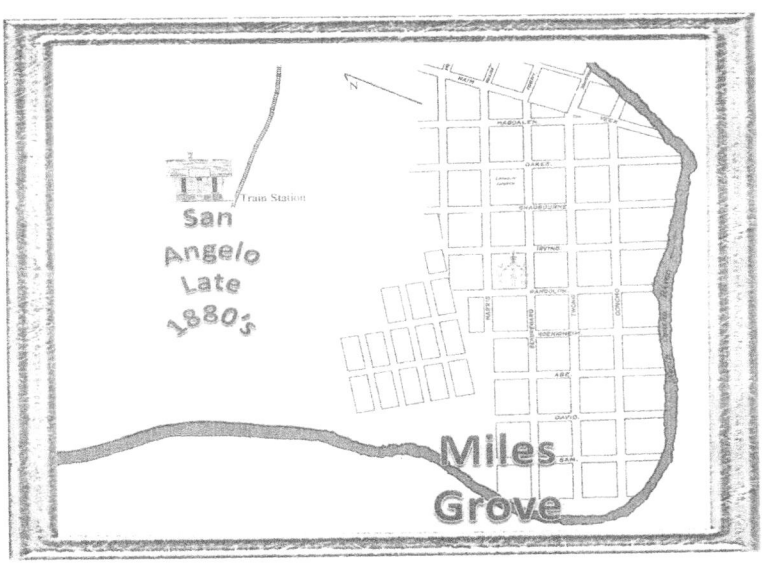

San Angelo Late 1880's

Train Station

Miles Grove

CHAPTER 10

1885 Awaken Dr. Bell

July 1, 1885
San Angelo, Texas

Dear Dr. Alexander Graham Bell,

I am writing to you because you have influence over the deaf community—seeing as both your mother and wife are deaf, and you teach linguistics to the deaf. I recently had new shoes fitted by a young deaf boy, and his story is one that I think you should know.

Drake was born with normal hearing to a struggling couple here in West Texas. He survived scarlet fever, but lost his hearing when he was five. Now he is a robust orphan working at the Kindle Shoe Shop on Main Street here in San Angelo.

This letter is about more than one deaf person, actually. Deaf Rudy is also involved in this correspondence. He became friends with Drake during a shared adventure. Rudy comes from wealth and also lives in San Angelo.

The following is their story.

When Drake and Rudy were about twelve years old, they met in an unusual situation. Rudy was being taken by stage to Austin, Texas, where he would attend classes at the *Deaf and Dumb Asylum*. He was being escorted there by his father, who continually tried to teach his son to read lips and vocalize his words.

Rudy was a handsome youth, dressed fashionably and with a suitcase filled with everything necessary for a semester away from home. No one on the stagecoach gave him any thought, as being deaf isn't as noticeable as other differences. Little did the passengers know that Rudy wasn't the only deaf minority on the stage.

You see, Drake was riding atop the stage with the driver. No one paid much attention to Drake either, because he was dressed shabbily and was probably just *hired help*. Drake had the sympathy of the stage driver, though. Drake didn't know where he was going to end up, but he was taking a pleasure ride to whatever the world threw at him. He was tired of being homeless—shifting from place to place and asking for handouts in San Angelo. He thought he might work for the stage line or maybe the railroad.

All was well with the trip, until they got to Brady. Twenty miles southeast of Brady, a group of bandits held up the stage. In the process, Rudy's dad was injured so badly that he could no longer travel. So he was brought to a nearby homestead, and Rudy was to go on to boarding school without him. This was not Rudy's first time to travel to the academy. He'd been there before for a few semesters.

At one of the stage stops, Rudy and Drake eyed each other and innately knew they had a commonality. Drake was much better at verbalizing, since he'd been able to hear for the first five years of his life. Drake did not know the proper motions for American Sign Language (ASL), though he had made up his own sign language with his parents.

Rudy had picked up some ASL in the dorms of the *Deaf and Dumb Asylum*, much to his father's dismay. The asylum and his family were adamant about not using hand motion sign language—they depended wholly on oralism.

The two boys tried to communicate with each other and found it a bit difficult, since Drake had never been with anyone who knew true ASL. Drake had never even been to school, though he'd learned to read and write from his mother before she died.

Rudy, on the other hand, was born deaf. But his parents had had the means to have him educated by the best. His family had been relocated to San Angelo from Austin, as a result of his dad being involved in real estate. Rudy had spent a few semesters at the asylum and could read lips well.

To speed things up, the boys got paper and pencils—they conversed that way. Eventually, it became apparent that Rudy wanted to bring Drake to the asylum to covertly learn ASL.

I'm telling you this story because, from what I understand, you are very much against the use of ASL and would like all deaf persons to only learn to read lips. I wonder why they can't just learn both!

Rudy successfully got Drake enrolled in the school because of his father's influence. Besides learning lip reading and vocalization, Rudy was learning the trade of printing and Drake was learning to make shoes. For several months during their free time in the dorm, Rudy and the other boys taught Drake ASL. And Drake taught what he could, how to vocalize. Reading lips was something they all did whenever necessary, though there were difficulties.

As you know, you still have to grab the attention of the deaf in order for them to look at your lips, while you are speaking. And many men do not trim their mustaches properly—which makes looking at the lips nearly impossible. Some of the students need spectacles for they are near-sighted. How can they read lips if the relatively small lips are a blur?

Oh, the beauty of sign language is that it is big to look at. At first it is like learning French or Spanish. No doubt, it is another language all its own. I have begun learning it from Drake now that I have shoes being made by him.

Oh, forgive me. I got distracted from their adventure. Let me return to Rudy's and Drake's story.

When the semester was over, both boys took the stage back to San Angelo where Rudy's father was mending well. Rudy's father (Theo) took pity on the fate of Drake and let him stay with them until the asylum's next semester was to begin. Drake was beginning to feel very confident about making shoes. He asked if he could cleanup and do grunt work at the shoe shop and was granted something of an apprenticeship. Rudy stayed jobless but liked hanging out at the shoe shop. Theo didn't want Rudy to do any lower class work but was proud that Drake was taking his destiny into his own hands.

If Rudy could master lip-reading and vocalizing, he would be sent to fine schools to become an architect or engineer, Theo thought. Rudy wasn't certain of what he wanted to be, but he knew that he enjoyed being in the company of other deaf persons who knew and practiced ASL.

As time went on, they went back to Austin for another term at the asylum. It was Theo's plan that the semester would be the last for Rudy and Drake. The boys were tall and nearly ready for the real world.

I now fast forward to a picnic in San Angelo. Coincidentally the boys and I were present at the same function, though we didn't know each other at the time. Miles Grove on the North Concho River is a pleasant area of pecan trees. Many a picnic has been held there. The shade is remarkable. Anyway most families had brought their basket of fried chicken and biscuits. I had a pleasant lunch with my wife and small daughter. There was a big commotion across the way, and I saw that my wife turned to see what was going on. I then also turned to see.

Concho Folks

A man named John was choking on what turned out to be a chicken bone. Apparently, Drake was acutely aware of the distress from twenty yards away and ran to him. You see, Drake was able to read John's distressed lips saying, "Help, I'm choking."

How Drake knew how to dislodge the bone with his big squeeze is beyond me. Others had been patting John on the back to no avail.

Since John is a county commissioner, held in high esteem, everyone at the party was jubilant when the bone was dislodged. Drake became a hero. Theo and Rudy were so proud of him, I'm sure. The town had a new outlook on what a deaf and dumb person could do to be useful. I know that I was proud of him even though it was the first time I'd ever seen him.

Later at the same picnic I was complaining to my wife that my feet hurt. I had gained weight and my feet had gotten fatter as well. Do you know that Rudy (from afar) must have been eavesdropping on my conversation. Because he came over and verbalized and signed, that Drake could make some new shoes for me. I began to realize that reading lips from afar could have some advantages in the political arena. You see, I am a member of the Eighteenth Texas Legislature. I would love to know what my adversaries are cooking up across the room from me.

I will learn to read lips.

I am convinced that lip reading is a necessary skill for the deaf. But it doesn't hurt to know how to do it by those who can hear, too. But unlike you, I don't think that lip-reading and vocalization should be the *only* *things* taught to the deaf. My mother and father know German, French and English. They are fluent in three languages. I would like to be fluent in American Sign Language as well as English. I've given up on learning German and French. But I have reasons to learn sign language.

I decided to get the new shoes. When I got fitted for my them, I formally met Drake and Rudy. We conversed crudely about their adventure on the robbed stagecoach and their subsequent friendship. When I couldn't understand their verbalization, they instinctively tried to sign their thoughts to me. I was impressed. I marveled at their skills.

Upon getting my finished shoes the next week I asked if they could help me learn to lip read and sign.

You see, Dr. Alexander Graham Bell, my small daughter is deaf now from having the mumps this spring. If I send her to the asylum when she is older, I would not like for her to have to "sneak around" in the dorms to learn ASL. I would want for her to openly learn it from her teachers.

But according to the *Darwinist Perspective and the Milan Conference of Deaf Educators of 1880*, we are to avoid the language of sign. They don't even want deaf to marry each other risking more deaf people being brought into the world.

I will hire Drake and Rudy to help teach me, my wife and my daughter sign language. I don't want my daughter to be invisible to the general public. I don't want her to be ashamed of knowing how to communicate in the quite visible language of sign.

I don't understand how the son and husband of deaf women could have the idea that gesturing is an instrument of imprisonment. And that the people like Drake, Rudy and my daughter are not true Americans if they use ASL. You may have invented the telephone for the benefit of an admiring humanity, but your constrained views on the non-hearing persons, sicken me.

Lip reading is a convenience for those who can hear. It is not designed to be handy for the deaf. And knowing more than one language is admirable. Diversity is good!

Once again, I say, "Can't Drake, Rudy and my daughter learn oralism and manualism at the same time?"

My daughter will—even if I somehow have to teach her myself!

Do not suppress the use of sign language among the deaf.

Awaken, Dr. Bell. Awaken!

Sincerely. Mr. Franklin Foster

CHAPTER 11

1885 Dumbfounded Duo

My wife June and I enjoy secret, devilish activities. To name a few—we produce the best corn whiskey, run the loudest newly-wed shivarees and plan the most elaborate scavenger hunts.

We are also passionate about our San Angelo. The town disguises us as ordinary store operators most days. But we tease when we can and we love to joke—particularly with tenderfoots.

Newcomers, especially, don't know what hit them when we welcome them to town. We take it upon ourselves to roll out the red carpet with frolic.

Therefore, when the Majors arrived in March of 1885, we received them with our usual audacity. They didn't seem to appreciate our bluntness. In fact the duo stubbornly snubbed us.

We wondered if we had overstepped our bounds. *Had we made a grave mistake?* I thought.

Because as it turned out, they were our landlords—they were owners of all the businesses of our street, River Avenue. Once we realized their importance, we tried our best to be mild mannered. However, after they had been in town a week, we realized how little we knew about them. And we wondered what they might think of us. *Do they like us, or not? I reflected. Will they renege on our lease?*

We desperately wanted to know their personal facts.

"Do the Majors have any children?" I asked June after she returned to our store, from a visit with ladies, including Cheri Major.

"Oh, I don't know. She hemmed and hawed around every intimate question we asked her."

"Does she think you are nosy?"

"Perhaps she alludes that I'm a gossip. She might be taking precautions, just in case," responded June. "Have you found out anything about them by talking to Cleo Major?"

"Nothing so far, but I've invited them both to the shivaree for the Templeton's tonight. Maybe they'll warm up to sharing their family life with us after we toast the bride and groom."

"Let's hope so," sighed June.

The shivaree in the street went as planned. There was bell ringing, beating of pots and pans, pounding on the door, yelling, and the stomping of feet. Cheri and Cleo were in the boisterous group, too. But they were obviously not accustomed to the misbehavior kicking off the Templeton's married life.

The newlyweds probably had been settled in bed with plans of hanky-panky when they were interrupted; for Mr. Templeton (half clothed) came to the front door to ward off the crowd. But, he was then captured and his head was dunked in the horse trough—much to the dismay of his robed, crying bride. Cleo and Cheri didn't think well of it either, if the horror on their faces was any indication.

I slung Mr. Templeton on my shoulder and carried him to the nearest outhouse. Then I nailed the door shut with him inside. When five minutes of angry pounding had elapsed, we men jubilantly released him—happily hoisting him up on our shoulders—and brought him back to his bride.

June had since circulated glasses of our corn whiskey to the crowd. When all were equipped with our brew, toasts to the bride and groom erupted. Subsequently, everyone went home to leave the lovebirds alone.

As Cleo, Cheri, June and I walked in the dark, I asked, "Are your relatives still in San Antonio?"

"Why do you want to know?" Cheri invoked.

"That's not important right now," Cleo added.

Uncomfortable silence followed.

Finally, "To be honest, we just don't like small talk," Cleo concluded as they entered the Nimitz Hotel.

So, as June and I went on to our home above our store, we shook our heads in amazement.

"What is it with that couple?" she asked, dumbfounded.

The next evening, June and I were talking.

"Mr. Major wants all the merchants of our street to support each other. So, he asked me to invent two scavenger hunts for his tenants on the avenue. The *north-side*-street merchants will have clues for the north hill of the Twin Mountains. The *south-side* merchants will be looking for the same items on the south hill of the twin peaks," I said.

"Oh wonderful. We didn't scare the Majors off with the shivaree last night. And you are so talented with making riddles for scavenger hunts. He will really respect you, if he doesn't already," June said.

"Yes. I hope so. I've already chosen the items to be hunted. The list includes: a feather, a fossil, a yucca seed, an arrowhead, a y-shaped branch, something orange, amber sap, a thorny twig, a spider web and fire. According to the boss, the team that finds all ten the quickest will win a sash and a round of drinks at the Red Saloon."

June asked, "Do you need any help with the riddles for the ten things?.

"I don't think so. But listen to this riddle for *fire*. 'What grows when it's fed and dies when it drinks?'"

"That's a good one, Edward!"

"And June, 'What is a house of earthen string; its owner has a biting sting?'"

"The spider web!" she replied after a little bit of thought.

I was glad it wasn't too hard.

Accordingly, I came up with eight *more difficult* riddles as clues for the hunt.

My wife and I still knew nothing about the lives of our landlord. Nonetheless, we hoped that the puzzle might be solved when the shopkeepers enjoyed the catered picnic after the hunt.

During the next week, Mr. Major arranged for several wagons to transport the vendors to the twin buttes, located eight miles southwest of the courthouse. June made the sashes for the winners.

He paid me five dollars to come up with the clues and plant some arrowheads and fossils on the hills. I made the Morse Code Flags (to relate progress to Mr. Major) for both teams. I also trained Jake of the South and Louis of the North on usage of the flags.

Our landlord would be watching the activities while at the foot of the hills. To win, a team would have to be first in making fire and turning in their nine items to the chief.

On the day of the event, the Majors, June and I greeted our business neighbors when they reached the camping spot between the two hills. The caterers had set up everything very elegantly. It was clear that the Majors were extremely wealthy people.

My friends, as two teams, climbed their respective hill with a sealed clue-envelope and two code flags per team.

Concho Folks

Mr. Major and I were excited about the teams. I worried that I made the clues too hard—or too easy.

The caterers were scurrying around making sure everything was just right. Ice blocks from Abilene kept the beer kegs and fried chicken cold.

During the competition June, once again, tried to tap Mrs. Major of information about her family. "Everyone likes to talk about their children," she exclaimed to me the night before.

June is persistent, I thought.

Cleo Major was using his binoculars to check on the flagman of each team. South had found eight and had fire's smoke. North had found seven and had not made fire yet. Within thirty more minutes the south team was cautiously making its way down the hill with all nine of its items. When it seemed that South would win, smoke rose from the north hill, too and their flags denoted ten items found. It became a slip, sliding race to the bottom of each hill. All members of the two teams were running neck to neck towards Cleo.

Amongst the chaos, June came rushing toward me flapping her arms up and down to get my attention.

"They don't have any children because they've only been married a month," she gasped for breath. "They were nervous about our reputation for pranks so they have kept quiet about themselves," she shouted.

June's yelling somehow got everyone's attention. It got relatively quiet as all the team members were just as curious about their proprietors as June and me. It seemed that no one had really gotten to know them.

Cheri also ran—running to her husband, with tears streaming down her red face.

"Our secret is out!" Cheri said to him quietly upon his embrace.

The Majors looked horror-struck.

I calmly got Mr. Major's attention with my somber face. "I would never prank my landlord, sir," I exclaimed (with my crossed fingers carefully hidden behind my back.)

"We respect your wishes and will not have a shivaree for you," I continued.

Cleo consoled Cherie as best he could.

With June at my side I said, "Let us truly welcome you to San Angelo with a toast of cold beer."

All of the teams, by then were down the hill and were no longer concerned about the contest. Most had been curious about whether or not their leases would be renewed, too.

Moments later, with beers in hand, everyone faced the Majors with admiration and respect.

After the salute, Mr. and Mrs. Cleo Major unexpectantly awarded all their tenants *one month's free rent*.

There was a big *hooray*. Then everyone ate and had a great time for the rest of the time on the prairie.

It was that day, that June and I finally understood the elusive Major puzzle.

Decoding the Majors had been no minor feat.

CHAPTER 12

1886 Freedom Figure

Since anything said with a Spanish accent could be used against you in 1886, bilingual Henry spoke perfect English in public. He was playing solitaire in the ballroom of the Magnolia Hotel in Seguin, Texas. Henry was about to be en route to San Angelo, Texas, where he had business with land management. But the stage and accompanying wagon carrying some of his personal effects were horribly late. It had rained overnight, and mud made an *on-time* stage as rare as a blue rose.

Henry was a ridiculously wealthy New Yorker who had inherited acreage near a red arroyo of San Angelo. He of late felt the need for its inspection. The only reason he didn't just sell the land upon coming into it was because he was insatiably greedy. If he could retain the property and make more money than its current worth, he would.

He would determine the land's fate soon, then back to New York he would go.

James, his traveling butler, had left him at the hotel temporarily to check on the stage's tardiness.

"You stupid butler, I've been ready to travel for ages." When the transportation finally arrived, Henry verbally clobbered James.

James retorted, "It's not my fault it rained last night!"

"I didn't say it was your fault, I said I was blaming you! Now let's get on with this trip," shouted Henry.

Later, James was writing in his journal and Henry was napping when the stage came to an unexpected halt. Abruptly awakened, Henry scolded the driver, "What's wrong, stupid?"

"Apparently if a horse can get hurt, it will," responded the driver, as he dismounted the stage. He checked the right front shoe of the limping horse.

"Use the nippers, and let's get this show on the road!" shouted Henry.

There was some eye-rolling amongst the hired hands. "I'm not bossy, I just know what you should be doing," said Henry from inside the coach. He was always repulsed with the help.

Instead of the nippers, the man used a rasp to bevel a splitting hoof. They were about to be on their way again when Henry just couldn't contain himself. "I'm never wrong. There are just different levels of right," he said.

All of the employees nodded in pseudo-respect as they maintained the animals. In a half hour, they were back to inching their way to San Angelo—the horses as compliant as puppets.

Because Henry went back to sleep, James resumed journaling. *I like the sound of Henry not talking,* he wrote. *And he likes it when I'm silent, too—but only because he thinks that I'm listening. Oh, the stress of that man. Too bad punching Henry would be frowned upon.*

Meanwhile, Henry dreamt of the specter of the Virgin Mary he'd seen at the Magnolia Hotel the previous night. The shadows had played tricks on his mind, as the wall had no apparition that morning. Nevertheless, Henry was a bit anxious. He secretly owned an unusual feather with the Madonna and baby Jesus on it. He was an atheist, but his protective feather was very important to him.

When arriving at their destination, the Nimitz Hotel of San Angelo, Henry's crew was not greeted with ease. Instead, there was a lot of tension in the air. And during the hottest part of the late day, a brawl began on Concho Avenue.

The scuffle began as Manny (an aging, short Mexican man) performed a maneuver on a choking Mexican friend. The freed morsel flew into the face of a passing Anglo. Anyway, that was the Mexicans' story. The Anglos didn't see it that way. They thought it was a free-for-all food fight with the Mexican tamale vendor as the scapegoat. But what started out as dinner slinging soon became fists hitting flesh like hammers on nails.

Henry and James stepped out of the hotel to see a ruckus—which was growing by the second. It was Anglos versus Mexicans in what was probably, the town's biggest riot since the days of the Comanches.

James said, "This fight isn't any of our business."

Henry countered, "I'd agree with you, but then we'd both be wrong. I'm ready to fight."

James replied, "Be careful when you follow the *masses*—sometimes the *"M"* is silent."

"It looks like fun, and I also don't care what you think—so it works out," Henry held, and then added, "But due to personal reasons, I won't be holding myself accountable for my actions."

So Henry barreled into the mob. He pulverized a Mexican and then crippled an Anglo. He was agile as he latched onto two opposing men and smashed their heads together. Then he invaded an empty wagon and pounced down into another group of jerks.

Several men, both Anglos and Mexicans, pressed forward into the crowd, as standing by during a good fight wasn't on their dance cards. A left assault to Manny collapsed him. This elderly man going down didn't go unnoticed, but everyone mauled each other anyway.

Manny's relatives snagged him to safety somehow and handed him his comforting statue. All the while the foray continued.

For being a rich guy, Henry didn't fall prone to the attacks as James had assumed that he would. At one point, Henry slugged a man so hard that the injured bolted towards his horse and loped off into the sunset.

All this was happening as James was just standing around being as benign as peppermint.

The law hollered for the scramble to end, but the men continued to bloody each other's noses and blacken each other's eyes.

Finally the sheriff and deputies opened fire at the sky, which caused most men to sprint or cower to safety.

"What the hell is going on here?" bellowed the sheriff.

It was a dumb question to ask, since, for several weeks, the Mexican squatters were being evicted by seven landowners. With no place to settle their families and no money to escape, the tension was as thick as the scrubby mesquite. The Anglos had gotten their attention, but the bushwhacked Mexicans had no choice but to rebel.

With the fight over, the Mexicans were expelled to the outskirts of town, and Henry was seen by the overworked doctor. After recuperating overnight, Henry was ready to meet the squatters on his land and expel them, too. He wore his baggiest clothes, since he was swollen from head to toe. He was telling James of his day's agenda at the shantytown.

"Your secrets are safe with me—I wasn't even listening," responded the butler.

Traveling with his henchmen and James, Henry came upon his parcel of land. At the red arroyo, flies were sometimes the first indication that something had died. But this early July day, the flies were hovering over a large display of vegetables that had disguised themselves as *human heads*. Pumpkins, squash, gourds, and melons were picked before the Latinos' departure from their previous seven shantytowns and were now resting in the shade of a hackberry tree. Clearly the community was gearing up for a contest of sorts—to ease their melancholy.

They never could have known of Henry's soft spot. You see, Henry's brain had a bias, favoring *seeing signs and portents,* rather than nothing—in ordinary things. His brain loved to jump to a pattern that made sense of a situation; hence, his feather with the Madonna image.

"Wow, what a wonderful set-up you have here," he said to no one in particular. The peasants had seen his kind before—flattery was an insult in gift wrapping. They knew what he was up to.

Manny, yesterday beat to smithereens, voiced, "Spare some change, please?" to Henry and his cohorts. Some of them no doubt had been the source of his troubles the day before. Manny had a small cloth bag. The donated shiny, new coins clanked on his metal statue when they entered the bag. The riders felt they'd done their good deed for the day.

But the midday sunshine in the rough neighborhood made the riders apologetic of the miserable atmosphere. They saw makeshift houses of crates and discarded metal—and small fires cooking tortillas and beans. Scantily dressed munchkins darted about, afraid of the strangers. Women gathered their babies, and men resumed their combative posture from the preceding day.

These people had the inner strength to eat the same food day after day—and be grateful for it. They could take criticism and blame without resentment. But something they could not change about their life was the poor, lower class into which they'd been squeezed.

They did not and would not have the endurance to move their ailing families again. And they were sure that was exactly what Henry intended for them to do. There was no other land on which they could squat available close enough to their city and fort jobs.

Some brilliant Mexican hidden, from Henry shouted in Spanish, "The real measure of your wealth is how much you'd be worth if you lost all your money."

Alarmed eyes widened.

Little did the man know that Henry was bilingual and understood every word. Henry could see that he had to make a difficult compromise in order to succeed.

But would the land have much monetary value if I sold it? he thought. *Would a fight with this blended community, already ousted by seven different landowners, be feasible?*

Just three months prior in Mexico, it took five thousand soldiers to capture Geronimo, twenty-four warriors, and their women and children. Henry made a rough estimate that he was dealing with hundreds of displaced and angry Mexicans. He and his ruffians numbered six—seven if you counted cowardly James.

"Just because I don't care, doesn't mean I don't understand," replied Henry.

If it was possible, the Mexican men stood even taller. "We just can't move again," Manny said in Spanish.

Breaking the tension, Henry was then asked to be a judge in the *vegetable human heads* contest.

Manny and Henry shared a modest meal after the contest and were settling in for the evening. Manny seemed to be the spokesperson for the clans.

It was July Fourth, and many Anglo families had gone to Lone Wolf for fireworks. It was also customary to blow up stumps on the holiday. The dogs of the township were due for some anxiety.

When it was nearly dark, Henry dug out of his pocket a deck of cards. He thought he'd teach his new friend Manny the game of solitaire. Five minutes into the game, a jack of clubs showed up in the dealer deck. Henry needed a red jack to put below a queen of spades. "I don't understand," Manny remarked, as Henry drew another card.

"It was the wrong color," said Henry.

"Just like my people and I are the wrong color," he countered.

Henry's face collapsed as if a pricked balloon.

Manny's hand went into and out of the cloth bag, retrieving nothing—as a loud explosion shook the ground and air. *Was there a pistol in there,* he thought.

Apparently one of the stumps being removed was on the edge of Henry's land. Screams ensued as some bloodied women and children came running from the north sector. The Anglos had chosen that stump with a vendetta in mind.

Manny was silent—standing before Henry as a little statuesque figure—yet internally he was screaming for freedom.

"Please sir, forget the disarrayed cards and promise me you won't make us move." The civility had changed to terror in Manny's voice. "No one of your figure has ever become poor by giving. And once you need less, you will have more," he concluded.

Another blast of dynamite boomed in the further distance. It was as if the neighboring land owners had decided that the *Mexican island* was easy target practice on the festive night.

Henry melted as if Manny's statements were a lame child's only wish. He reached in his own bag with the sacred feather and pulled out some paper to make some legal statements about the property. He would finalize the transactions at the Tom Green County Courthouse in coming weeks.

All the while, explosions kept the dogs running wild as the night dragged on.

Before Henry left, Manny pulled from his own tattered bag a metal treasure he'd received in a trade for a catering job.

A statue—

Not the Virgin Mary as some might have suspected—but a six-inch symbol of another lady.

It was a freedom figure called Lady Liberty.

Henry was honored when Manny gave it to him.

Epilogue

The Mexican people received surveyed lots to call their own from Henry.

In October, Henry returned to New York.

His ship from Galveston passed the dedication of the brand-new Statue of Liberty.

Though still an atheist, he continued to tightly grip the bag containing both his feather of Madonna and Manny's figure.

While on his ship, near her island, he saluted the majestic Lady Liberty.

But he knew in his heart that it would take many decades (maybe even centuries) for the *filth of racism* to diminish everywhere.

Shaker Broom Vise

CHAPTER 13

1886 The Day Sleeper

Until her thirteenth birthday, Graciela had been pampered. But when Father passed away, the forthcoming stepfather challenged the lenient discipline in the house. With *his* debut, Graciela no longer would be cultivated into a princess. This is a story of how the guarded girl got into a crude predicament in San Angelo, Texas.

Jim, her stepdad had told her to gather broom weed from the pasture and bring bundles of it to the broom-maker on Concho Avenue. She saw her dynasty crumbling with this command. She was confident, but never went out in public. That day, she certainly didn't want to be outdoors gathering plants.

It had been that petty chore that had brought spoiled Graciela into her scratchy situation.

Jim had arranged for Graciela to deliver the bundles to the broom shop on Sunday morning; when most people were at church. Upon letting herself into the broom establishment, she heard the heavy door close on itself. When the corroded door latch wouldn't give to her efforts, she realized that she'd become a prisoner in the small factory.

She would need church services to be over, in order to regain her freedom. As she waited, she sat on the floor near her bundled broom weed and considered crying. It was during this annoyance that she realized she wasn't alone.

First, there were itchy things in her clothing—and secondly, there was someone else in the room!

She scratched at her waist and the top of her leggings.

Chiggers! How maddening, she thought.

But also in the chamber with her, there was snoring, timeworn woman using the clamping vise as a pillow.

Well, thought Graciela, *there's no need to wake her.* As ancient as the broom maker looked, even she and Graciela together wouldn't be able to open the door.

The old woman didn't budge. The elder must have fallen asleep right there—while sewing the broom in the vise.

In due course, it didn't matter that she wasn't alone, because Graciela began to undress near a bucket of drinking water. *A damp rag of cool water on the chigger bites would bring relief,* she thought. She had time to tend to her rashes.

She had stripped to her petticoat and bodice, determined to rub away the invaders, when the clock struck the half hour—and the woman began to stir.

"Please excuse me," Graciela said as she ran half naked to a dark corner.

"Who goes there?" asked the waking octogenarian.

"I brought the broom weed that Jim prescribed. I've become locked in here with you. I am so sorry to alarm you."

Graciela, in her haste, had left her clothes near the water bucket.

The surprised elder had dropped the huge double pointed needle she'd been using. While the grandma fumbled around feeling for it, Graciela dashed to her clothes; grabbed her leggings, then retreated back to her dark corner.

"I say, girl, would you be as kind as to open a window. It is rather sultry in here during this Indian summer."

"Ma'am, I would, but I am too frail due to my cold," Graciela lied.

"Girl, do you have a fever?"

"My mother has been nursing me with hot teas. But my mean stepfather insisted that I deliver the broom weed here. I'm allergic to it, you know—I'm sure of it. He is so hateful."

Finding her needle, the elder continued stitching the broom.

"I can survive the humidity, so no worries about the window."

Just then a pet cat meowed near Graciela. "Are you allergic to cats, as well? I hope not," the grandma asked.

The insincere girl became melodramatic in her response. "No. I have cats of my own. They generally give me a nonchalant stare. I would rather not have any animals. They are crude and probably make me sick. Come to think of it, I probably *am* allergic to cats."

Grandma finished stitching the broom and brought it to the broom slicer to make a straight edge. The cutter made a sickening noise.

Graciela was certain that the elder knew she was poorly clad in the shadowed corner. "Truthfully, the chiggers in the field found their way into my clothes," she said modestly. She pointed to her pile of clothes near the drinking water bucket and hunched down to the floor in a fetal position. "My awful day started off with my hitting my pinky toe on the coal stove. Then my stockings kept sliding down into my shoes. At some point, I was telling a story to my mother when I realized—she wasn't even listening."

"And you caught a cold, little one?" the grandma asked as she helped herself to a dipper of cool water from the bucket. Inches away from her feet were the girl's shoes and dress. The girl silently shook her head.

Then the elder turned away and went back to the broom making station. There she gathered broom weed to make another broom.

"I must say, it is embarrassing to be in this predicament," commented Graciela. "Only my mother has seen me in my undergarments."

"Well my son will be back from church shortly, so it is best that you tidy up."

Graciela hesitantly went to the bucket and finished getting dressed. She was still itching horribly. But with the proprietor of the factory due any minute, she had no time to relieve the irritation.

Graciela was ready to go home.

"I've never seen you before. Have you only just moved to San Angelo?" asked the girl.

"No. I've lived here for several years. I just don't get out much," said the grandma.

The octogenarian continued binding broom weed to a long stick. "Some people who have seen me think I should be flying the brooms I make. They think I mix up strange brews from toad and lizard tongues. They probably think I could cure you of your cold."

"Oh, I don't really have a cold, or fever. I just didn't know how to explain why I was half naked in your shop," Graciela held. "Do you fall asleep often?"

There was silence in the room. The elder seemed to have dozed again. Perhaps she had a sleeping disorder. Graciela patiently waited for her to wake up.

Upon the owner's arrival into his shop, the grandma woke.

Graciela was about to leave when she heard the grandma say, "Dear son, please untangle this string for me. Sometimes it's so difficult being blind."

Graciela's slight smile became a frown as she thought, *what must it be like to be blind.*

Abruptly, she turned and walked toward the old woman. "Here, let me get that. While her hands picked at the string, she felt different—as if the tangled thoughts complicating her view of the world, somehow became less so.

For like a sweeper, the independent woman had swept Graciela to a different place. The grandma's proverbial broom appeared to have cleaned out negative thoughts in the greedy girl.

That day, and days thereafter, were a series of new beginnings for the teenager. Remarkably, even chores brought about a new sense of satisfaction.

Especially sweeping—

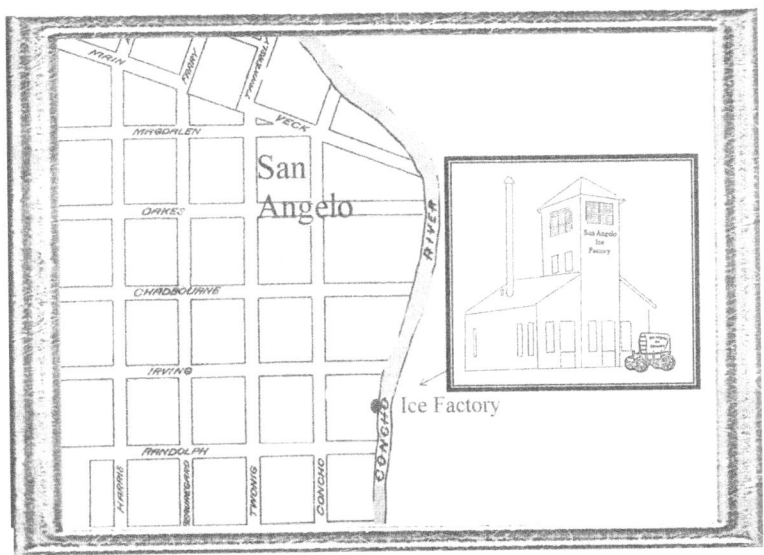

CHAPTER 14

1886 The Mutt

M ay 1886
Fort Worth, Texas

Dearest Penny,

Enclosed is my translation of Father's last letter to us. I know your German and Spanish are not strong; that's why I decoded it for you. Our father finally has a job! I'll let you find out for yourself. But now we can be upset for other reasons.

Love,

Cecile

April 24, 1886

Dear daughters,

Thank you for the birthday present last month. I had forgotten that I am now a fifty-year-old mutt. My leg deformity from that cowboying incident still gets me down sometimes, but all in all I'm getting around OK as long as I have my bourbon. I've had some pretty good years. The births of you two girls were the highlight of my life.

My birthday was uneventful, as San Angelo is having an epidemic of chicken pox right now. It happens every spring, it seems. Most of the ill kids are bedridden. So I get a lonely kind of feeling when I walk along the streets. Oh, the dreariness will pass soon.

I have a job at the San Angelo Ice Factory! I'm a part-time day helper and a full-time night watchman. It's not easy with my handicap, but everyone understands. It takes me a while to climb the stairs to check pressure gauges and such, but I can still do it. They wish I didn't have my flask of whiskey, but they don't know what it takes to get me through the day.

My night vision is worsening. Fortunately we have oil lamps installed throughout the factory. My peripheral vision seems to be getting smaller and smaller. I suspect it has been happening slowly as of this year, for I used to be able to see the left and right corners of my tenement room at the same time. I know this because once, my two mouser cats were in each corner while I was standing in the doorway. I know that I could see them both at the same time. They were conversing with each other across the room. Now if I see one corner, I cannot see the other and vice versa. It is so frustrating to be like this. I wonder if there are spectacles for my kind of problem. Will you look into that for me? I don't trust Texas doctors, since the one who set my leg did it wrong.

Will you tell your children that working in the Ice Factory is good, respectful work? We pump and distill the Concho River. We have operations for cooling distilled water in the big freezing tank. This is how we make ice (which is half the price of imported blocks) in San Angelo.

First, we have a wood-burning firebox that heats water in the boiler for steam power. With that power, we are constantly moving, compressing, and expanding three fluids: water, ammonia, and oil. Each of these needs to be cooled with water-condenser baths. The water that was filtered and distilled then becomes ice. The ammonia circulates within large and small-diameter pipes, some of which are submerged in very salty water (which is the freezing tank). The tank is where the ice molds temporarily sit to freeze. The oil circulation keeps all of the moving parts lubricated and maintains a vacuum. It is very rewarding to see the water from the North Concho River being turned into crystal-clear, distilled ice chunks with this factory.

Because the ice is crystal clear, it takes a while for it to melt. But it also takes a while for it to freeze. The molds for the ice are rectangular. When they are frozen to the middle, we dunk the molds in tepid water and remove the ice. Then, of course, we refill the molds for the next batch of ice. The ice brick weighs about one hundred pounds. Oh, for a man my age, moving the masses around is a chore. The floor can get pretty slippery, too if you don't pay attention. There is always some waste ice. So the broom is my friend during the daytime. I prevent slipping accidents.

Most of the ice is used by breweries and saloons, though we supply to ice cream shops as well. We also have a horse-drawn wagon for ordered sales. The ice wagon goes to businesses and residences to deliver chunks of ice.

There is a group of women (The Temperance Society) that is very much against the ice factory. They don't want anyone to drink alcohol—period. They claim that ice should only be made for food preservation and ice cream. ("Forget the beer," they say.) Those women apparently don't have pain in their leg, as I do. I must have my beer every afternoon.

We have been fortunate that our setup has only been running for one year. It has had few breakdowns because of its newness. Other, older factories haven't been so lucky. I worry about mechanical failure all the time. I'm not a very smart man, and I don't understand everything that maybe I should. But I know explosions can happen, and I don't want to be around when it occurs. I'm glad the clever people can understand the internal conditions of the machinery by looking at gauges; then they know how to respond. The gauge for the pressure within the steam engine is my biggest concern. Otherwise, we mostly just reliquefy and re-evaporate the ammonia over and over again. And did I mention that ammonia is explosive? Well it is. But don't have fear about it!

I know you worry about me, but I feel safe. My nighttime job entails listening for unusual noises and making sure that no one vandalizes the place. Last summer was the first season for San Angelo to have an ice factory, and my boss was surprised at how many people wanted to come into the ice room to recuperate from the excessive heat outside. The night watchman, at the time, had to run off several persons of questionable character—and even some of good character. Did they think the factory had opened an ice hotel or something?

I myself have slept on the floor of the ice room on occasion this spring. It feels so comfortable in the heat of the season to sleep in a cold room with lots of blankets on me. I can drink my bourbon to warm up occasionally and just let the two cats snuggle with me. Most other people are sleeping with their windows open, with mosquitoes biting, and with no relief from the constant sweating. I sleep like a lamb.

Today is the Saturday before Easter Sunday, and we are actually making ice at night this one time. There was a big influx of ice orders because of all of the celebrating going on, so we are running the machinery tonight. I'm feeding the fire in the firebox. In the morning a crew of men will come in before church and get the ice to where it has been ordered.

I had an *epiphany moment* the other day when I was sweeping the ice scraps off the floor, into the tepid water tank. I thought, *I can save bits and pieces of ice and sell it to my favorite saloon.*

I'd been trying to use my brain to come up with the scheme successfully. Two days later, my boss found me drawing the "ice box" I was going to build for the endeavor. I flinched when he asked me what it was. I said it was a toy for my granddaughter. He smiled and went on with his day. I don't know if he knew I was thinking of my own side ice business with the waste of his factory. So far, I've made the box, and it is in the ice room looking innocent. No one suspects me, as far as I know.

The problem with starting my own business from the icehouse waste is—probably every other guy has thought of the same thing. For all I know, someone is already making money for himself—as I plan to. Is it a sin? Will he go to hell for doing it? What if he never gets caught?

Oh, you see that I'm frustrated with my pay as part-time day and night watchman. I don't have enough money to buy as much whiskey as I need. I know you don't approve of the juice, but it helps me with the loss of your mother, too. Anyway, in order to drink, I need to find a better job or smooch off the side.

This shift tonight has been curious because while I'm writing this, I'm intermittently adding wood into the firebox of the steam engine to keep the ammonia and oil circulating (so the water freezes for Easter). Also, this evening I had three interesting visitors: Paul, an orphan; exciting Candace, the temperance lady; and Mutt, the pregnant dog.

I'll start with Mutt's giving birth to two female puppies, while the cats and I looked on. I just randomly named her Mutt as she seems to be a stray dog. I won't bore you with the disgusting details of the procedure, but she labored for quite a while, and I was with her the whole time. I couldn't help but remember when your mother gave birth to you two sisters. Oh my, how I miss your mother!

Candace the exciting temperance lady was standing outside of the front door until dark. She had a sign on a stick which read, *Alcohol causes sin!* When I first saw the logo, I kind of took it personally. But some of the other society members have been stationed outside the saloons with their own signs and their own individual slogans. I eventually rationalized she wasn't aiming her message at me but rather at the ice being made for breweries and saloons.

The reason I find Candace to be exciting is because she is precisely opposite of your mother in the way she looks and the way she acts. It is strange that I'm attracted to anyone, even though your mother has been dead for eighteen years. Don't worry that I'm going to marry her or anything like that. I just had a little spark *light up* in me today, which I haven't felt for a very long time. Can you imagine me not drinking alcohol? Ha!

My last little visitor is another mutt of sorts called Paul. He is about seven years old and has recently been ditched by his *supposed* aunt. His harlot mother died last year. He is remarkably resilient, considering he sleeps in Nasworthy's Stables and begs for food the rest of the time.

Anyway, Paul has the chicken pox, and he is so feverish that he instinctively came to the coldest place he could think of. I have on occasion given him scraps of food to help him through his day. On some of the cold spring nights, I've even let him (with the boss's approval) sleep in the office in the warm bed the factory provides for me, whilst I slept on the floor. Tonight I am letting him sleep wherever he is most comfortable. If he has chills, it's under the covers. If he is hot, it's to the freezing room. I'm testing to see if the brine water might help with the itching. I don't think it works. I even tried smearing bourbon on the sores, but the open ones stung like wasps, so I quit right away. By the time you get this letter, he should be over the pox. I feel so sorry for the kid. He is going through hell right now.

This is the end of my letter, as I cannot think of anything else to talk about. But would you consider having a little brother the same age as your own children? When I see little Paul all ragged and miserable, I think that maybe I could be his adoptive father. I could help someone other than myself. Let me know what you think. I might even ask my boss if we can keep Mutt (the dog) as a watch dog. I love you both!

Your Father,
Viktor Gunther

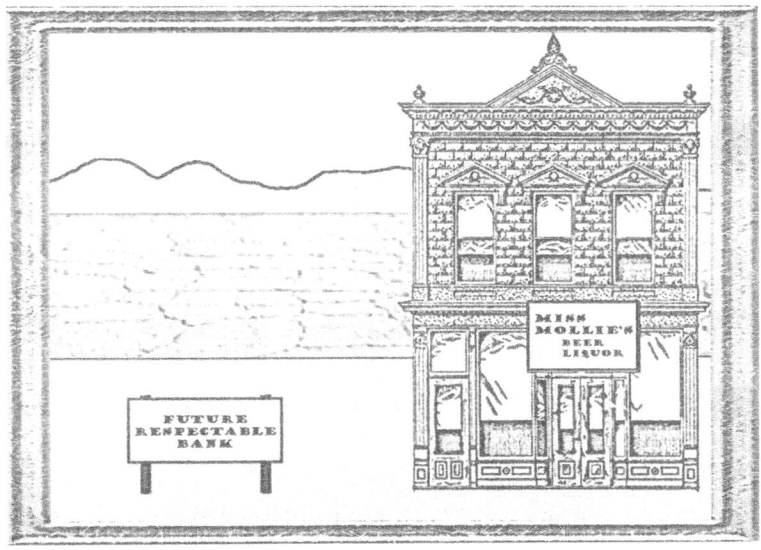

CHAPTER 15

1887 Breaking the Bank

When in a hole, Buster usually thought of coffee. He'd been digging holes for a living, and he always thought about the coffee he'd soon drink. While down under, he dug and dug, inhaling dirt as he went.

Sometimes he'd come upon a huge boulder that quieted his progress. So he'd blast it to pieces with precision. But mostly he used a pick, shovel, and bucket to reckon with mother earth while he waited for another pot of black, liquid Joe.

No doubt, Buster loved coffee.

He had been raised on substitute coffee made from roasted dandelion root. Upon leaving his childhood home, he found out about real coffee beans—and would never go back to the root tea. He might be a simple earth mover, but buying real coffee beans wouldn't break the bank.

By trade, Buster dug wells and anything else underground. He was now excavating a basement below Miss Mollie's Saloon. Miss Mollie was adamant about having a storm cellar—she was sick with worry, because her town was recovering from a tornado. The storm had stripped the cupola off the courthouse and created havoc throughout the town of several thousand.

So there was Buster beneath the saloon, with a bucket needing to be raised. "Hurry up," shouted Buster to his partner, Gus, who was on the first floor receiving the bucketed rubble.

"I'm working as fast as I can!" Gus replied. Buster was so revved up on coffee that Gus couldn't move quickly enough.

Patience was a virtue that both men lacked, and they each had their own agenda.

"You two quit fussing—it's almost time to open the saloon!" Miss Mollie yelled from the kitchen.

She'd been making a fourth pot of coffee as the commotion and dust came visiting. She'd just about had it with the invasion of the two working men at her place. However, she knew the inconvenience of the digging would be worth it in the end. "Gentlemen, come here and get some coffee. That's enough clamor for the day," she said.

She then asked her daily question, "Are y'all almost done with the basement?"

The men scowled, as this woman was unrealistic about their speed. She only wanted them to dig from 7 a.m. to 2 p.m. About the time they began making progress, she desired them to quit for the day.

She was hopeless. They drank their coffee and left.

And so it was that Buster and Gus would shift from their basement job at Miss Mollie's to their other job next door at a *bank-yet-to-be*. Though they liked looking at the pretty waitresses at their Miss Mollie job, they enjoyed the fresh air at their bank job better. The Security

Bank had land next to Miss Mollie's and decided to have a basement as well. But the bank hadn't been built yet. So it was much easier to hollow out a hole in the ground there, than at Miss Mollie's.

Buster reflected on Miss Mollie while drilling into rock at the bank's basement. If he didn't know better, Miss Mollie might have a little crush on him. And for most men that would be a grand compliment, as Miss Mollie could have any man in town that she wanted. But Buster had sworn off women because of a hard breakup three years prior. He'd not been with a woman since that time, and he wasn't going to start now. Miss Mollie was a beautiful woman, always dressed in red. Many men visited the saloon for social reasons. Buster was not one of them.

"I'm more comfortable at the General Store drinking coffee," Buster told Gus once. "I'm saving my money so I don't have to dig holes anymore. I want to be a freighter out in the open air with mules and a wagon."

Gus remarked, "But you don't have mules or a wagon."

Buster replied, "I will when I finish these two basements! Shortly I'll have enough to buy all that I need for my new occupation. Soon I won't be digging root cellars and dugout homes anymore. Just wait and see, Gus."

Well, that was how it would be. Buster had been frugal with his money for years and was about to see the rewards of being so economical. But it should be mentioned that Buster could be unreasonably stingy. Here is an example of the extent to which Buster would go to save money for his dream.

One day, he noticed that his coffee grinder wasn't working because the bolt's nut had loosened and gotten lost. You would think he could just go to the General Store and get another nut for the grinder. Or maybe he could just buy a new grinder, seeing as they do eventually wear out. But this is what Buster did instead.

When Miss Mollie wasn't in her kitchen one morning, he took her coffee grinder and quickly brought it to his shack. In his mind, he thought he had borrowed it temporarily.

Now, why would he do that?

He was making about forty dollars per month with expenses of ten dollars per month. So he was saving thirty dollars per month for the wagon and mules. You'd think he could spare a couple of dollars for a new grinder, since coffee was a big staple of his diet.

Well, when Miss Mollie realized that her grinder was gone, she first accused everyone in hearing distance. When no one fessed up, Miss Mollie reported the theft to the local newspaper, the *San Angelo Standard Times*. Without success in getting it back, she then went to the store and bought another one.

Buster, on the other hand, had two grinders—one working and the other missing a nut. He planned to return her grinder when he found the lost nut. Buster made his delicious coffee with Miss Mollie's grinder, and no one was the wiser—not even Gus. Because if you have a secret, it only remains a secret if you tell *absolutely no one.*

The two basements were progressing; the bank's was finished before Miss Mollie's because of the ease of its construction. The bank's basement was already complete when Miss Mollie's basement hit a snag. Well, it wasn't a snag as much as a big, conglomerate boulder. There were several on River Avenue where the two establishments were located. They say that when you're overconfident and rushed, you have an accident.

And that's exactly what happened to Buster.

Buster was just days from finishing the second basement; therefore, he was days from beginning his dream job. He'd already had his eyes on buying mules and a wagon from the nearby livery stable.

So when Buster went to the store to get gunpowder and cannon fuse for the blowout, you could say that he kind of overdid it. He'd had eight cups of coffee that morning and wasn't up to making serious decisions. He used poor judgment in the amount of gunpowder he would use on the boulder.

The boom was louder than any that had been heard in the prior months. The cracking went all the way through the very large boulder. Buildings trembled as if there'd been an earthquake. People on the street scrambled to their homes. When the rubble had settled, Buster went back down in the hole.

"I'll put my head in and see what's inside," said Buster to no one in particular.

To make a long story short, the fragmented boulder was gradually removed by Gus. And eventually, Miss Mollie realized that they should keep digging in the direction of the vacated boulder.

Why? Because doing so would make a tunnel that would connect the bank basement to her basement.

She had talked to a bigwig of the bank, and they settled on having a tunnel between the buildings. Bank customers could use the tunnel to inconspicuously enter Miss Mollie's. Only some gentlemen were in the know about the tunnel, and most of the townspeople never realized it was there.

Now, why didn't Buster dig the tunnel?

Because he'd left town with his pay and belongings. He'd been embarrassed that he'd stolen the grinder and had frightened the town. Buster bought mules and a wagon in Ballinger and became a freighter.

But he also did something important before he left.

You see, the explosion shook Buster's shack a few blocks away from Miss Mollie's. When he went home after the distressing shockwave—*there*, in plain sight, was the missing nut. So Buster fixed his coffee grinder and anonymously returned Miss Mollie's to her kitchen.

Miss Mollie was surprised to see it when she came downstairs the next morning. She paid Buster and let him go.

Later, with Buster gone, Miss Mollie and Gus fell in love.

Gus worked at the bank next door, and Miss Mollie's Saloon business thrived.

And she could easily afford fifty coffee grinders.

CHAPTER 16

1888 Courting Fear

"And that is how I met my wife twenty years ago," concluded Jim to five other men in the room. They'd improvised a club where middle-aged men could get away from their wives for one evening a week. They discussed politics, the new railroad, the economy, and on this night—stories of their past. It was dark outside, but in the window a lantern and sign invited gentlemen to the meeting.

Lester was about to take a turn at a story when a knock on the door interrupted the gathering. A thin man humbly walked in. After brief introductions, Lester began his story as the men listened. But it didn't take long for the members to wonder about their newest recruit.

It was very noticeable that this new member was highly uncomfortable. He crossed one leg and then the other—over and over again. Lester and the other men finished their soliloquies, while he sat in the darkest corner of the room. Even though he'd been offered whiskey and a cigar, the ruddy man had declined. *Perhaps he is merely shy,* they thought.

When all the men had summed up their stories and events of the week, they looked to the stranger to see if he had anything to say. With trepidation he began a story.

"I fought in the Civil War and did something that has given me grief ever since," he said. "I fought against the Yankees in the Battle of Chickamauga in Tennessee. During the rage, I came upon a Union man already down, with his pocket watch in his hand. His eyes were open, but he appeared dead to me. I took the watch and chain, as I did not have a timepiece of my own. I didn't think anything of it. But later, when the war was over, I'd have memories of him *staring at me while I was taking his watch.* I should have closed his eyes prior to the theft."

"His image came and went for a few years and then as suddenly as the visions had come—they stopped."

"But as the twenty-fifth anniversary of that battle was arising this month, I began to see him in my dreams. I assured myself that I could ignore him and certainly time would heal this abrasion in my life—as it had before. But the apparitions began to show up in the day, too, as a shadow on the wall. Oh—that deathly face."

"I was unable to eat, for *fear* ransacked me. I became paranoid about when or where I would see his shadow next. Then, as you know, several days ago the city had the Grand Celebration for the newly completed railroad. During the parade I saw his total self in the crowd, and he stared at me. I had hoped I was mistaken, but there was no doubt about it when I saw him again at the barbecue at Miles Grove. He constantly glared at me. I did not want to miss the speech that afternoon, but I thought that maybe I should go back to my room and lay safely in my bed—I was so shaken by his relentless haunting."

"The evening of the ball at the courthouse, I decided that within the crowd of four thousand I could remain anonymous to this ghost.

I've been seeing a woman who desired that I dance with her at the party. I could not let her down. If I confessed my reasons, she would surely have laughed in my face."

"So she and I were in the courthouse dancing when I noticed him in the room, observing me intently. I began to recollect that with each of my sightings of him, he was appearing closer and closer to me, daring me to run wildly in fear with each subsequent glimpse.

At the dance we were only a few feet away from each other, and it was then that I noticed him looking at my—his—watch attached to my vest. That is when I knew he had lived and was hunting me down with revenge."

"I gave my apologies to my lady and planned to discharge from the nearest doorway. But he was **there**. When I went to the other three exits of the courthouse, he was at each. It was as if he had duplicated himself three times. *How can I escape?* I thought."

"I went up the stairs to hide in the courtroom. The doors were locked. I planned to proceed to the clock tower where surely his ghost would not follow. But I tripped on the stair landing and laid flat on my back."

"Though shaken, I was in the process of getting up when he was suddenly by my side, grabbing for my watch. I pushed him away, but he yanked my chain and then punched me in the nose."

"My next recollection was being in Doctor Smith's infirmary. I woke up in a bed, while he was saying, 'You've been asleep for three days.'"

"I only, just before coming here, stepped outside of his office and began wandering aimlessly. I am starving and distraught not knowing if I will see the monster again."

Everyone was on the edge of his seat, sick with worry for the man.

The hairs on the back of everyone's neck stood straight up when there was a knock at the door.

Not the Union soldier but the deputy walked in.

He made eye contact with the stranger.

"This man escaped from the jail this evening. I figured he might have accepted your sign's invitation."

"Back to jail you go, you rascal!" he said.

There was confusion in the room as the deputy handcuffed the man.

Upon leaving, the stranger faced the angry men and laughed.

"I made up that story when Lester was telling his."

Ha!

"I yanked *your* chain!"

CHAPTER 17

1888 Newsprint Genius

I am about to share the experience of my alarming encounter with Oscar. It is somewhat unbelievable and so you may not trust me, but I hope you will listen and treat it as truth. It all happened a year ago, when I was still very naughty. I'd been at my usual bar, hustling and drinking when I got out of hand and was taken to the Tom Green County Jail. There I met a *boy of a man* who altered my life. I'd been a renter and jack of all trades before meeting Oscar. But he and I became a team with good fortune soon after that wonderful night.

He was pimpled, tall and lanky when I first saw him in the jail. He was in rags, had head lice and smelt of an outhouse. I asked him why he was there but he gave no answer. There was something peculiar about him that I couldn't quite pinpoint—until we got to know each other in the coming months.

The jailer told me that Oscar was going through laudanum opioid withdrawal and that a traveling photographer from Lubbock County had dumped him at our jail. Sure enough he was sweaty, nervous, yawned frequently and seemed to be having diarrhea issues (if the chamber pot was any indication.) Goosebumps were on his arms even though it was a warm spring. The jailer said he hadn't slept for days and just paced the cell—over and over again. Also, he wouldn't eat.

These were small issues compared to what the jailer said next. It was understood that Oscar was the son of an important dead man and that there were henchmen of a senator out to quiet him, too.

I didn't understand why he needed to be quieted since he hadn't spoken a word while I was there.

The nomadic photographer had told the jailer, "Just wait till he starts talking again—he won't shut up!"

I became curious.

I was released from jail the next day with a stern warning to behave myself. Oscar, the boy in a man's body, became my obsession after my discharge. What was the mystery about him? How long would he need the jail to get over laudanum? Did he have any means of support? Was anyone really out to get him?

I went to visit him at the jail. I began to realize that he was mentally and emotionally challenged—but he could memorize anything he read—even if only seeing it once. When he did begin to talk, after withdrawal was over, he only uttered memorized lines.

He avoided eye contact with other humans and he *never made conversation*. He was a living, breathing source of huge amounts of information. He'd read newspapers and encyclopedias of which he'd recite upon request. He also, to my dismay, spoke voluntarily and *incessantly*.

What got him in trouble was that he'd read a shady senator's letters. This caused the informing photographer's gangster paranoia.

Concho Folks

Apparently a Texas senator by the name of Noel had written to Oscar's dad about some questionable deals concerning the formation of the XIT Ranch of the Texas Panhandle—the pact that financed the construction of the State Capitol in Austin. Oscar's dad of poor eyesight had his young son read the letters to him—not knowing that the letters would eventually become damning evidence against the senator. Then the senator sought Oscar. Oscar's dad returned the incriminatory letters back to the senator, but the senator still wanted Oscar—and his perfect memory, too.

So, I decided to protect Oscar from the senator's cronies. But in the meantime I also saw an opportunity for a symbiotic relationship between the two of us. I would clean and groom him to become a public speaker. I would promote the shows where he would recite prose requested by the crowds. I would charge a dime per person who attended the spectacles. We would become a wealthy, traveling sideshow.

At first I supplied reading material scrounged from debris. Eventually as we became richer, I'd buy newspapers that the audience seemed to want narrated. It was easy to prove to audiences that no trickery was occurring. I encouraged people to bring written text of their own liking and before the show started, he'd read their donations. As the show began and progressed, he would–on demand–wow the audience with his memory of the captions he'd only just read.

For instance, he described the newly opened Washington Monument in detail. Perfect explanations—of the new Statue of Liberty and the growing Eiffel Tower—amazed the crowds. The people loved him. I was getting attached to him, too—as I was becoming smarter and richer. Consequently, Oscar was the object of my extreme protection.

Therefore, you can imagine the horror I felt from a stalker one night at our roadshow in Austin, Texas. I'd been careful to put my face only—instead of Oscar's—on the publicity fliers throughout the state. I'd even hired my own muscle man to guard us against anyone from the senator's group. As it turned out, it was Oscar's good uncle who found us first. That was when I learned about the seriousness of the situation. If the uncle could find us, so could the senator.

We hightailed out of Austin and ventured back to San Angelo where we, with our muscle man, could breathe a little easier. Oscar, of course, wasn't *in the know* of his danger.

One day I asked him to recite the contents of the senator's letters and upon hearing their contents, decided to conceal him in Knickerbocker. We put our public appearances on hold—which turned out to be fine, since during our retirement, he contracted laryngitis.

I had forgotten what silence tasted like.

During his convalescing, I wrote letters to my parents in Kentucky and started planning our escape from Texas. We could resume our shows in the eastern states of the thirty eight states of America, soon. Our money wouldn't run out for a few months. We just needed to lay low for a while.

About that time, our muscle man left us—to go back to his wife—but we felt safe in the small town on Dove Creek.

But my life fell apart at the train station in San Angelo.

They took him from me! We were about to flee the state and resume our road show in Kentucky when he was abducted. As you can see me now, I am back to being a lonely jack of all trades.

Oscar is gone. The thugs may have killed him. Or they drugged him and hid him somewhere in the three million acres of the XIT ranch. He is probably high on laudanum again and talking constantly, as was typical.

I miss him! And I yearn for the road, too. The silence is golden, but now I have to turn an honest penny. And I'm back to being as dumb as a fish. A great pain grips my heart.

CHAPTER 18

1888 Liza's Lie

Whenever you see a bridge, you wonder if it is strong enough. At least that is what I would think (as a child) when we traveled across the rickety bridge on the way to grandmother's house. I would pray the Lord's Prayer during the jaunt across, to pacify my anxiety.

Though it seemed like we were going to fall to our deaths, my intercessions always saved my family. That bridge was on the short cut to grandmother's house. I always wanted to take the "long cut" without bridges—if you know what I mean. That bridge was a symbol of anxiety for me.

Fortunately, the bridge to grandmother's house has since been torn down and replaced. But when I was young, a unique bridge *story* was told to me, on one of those trips to see Grandmother.

The story's main character was Liza, and she was pregnant when she lived in San Angelo in 1888. That year was also the birth year of the town's *hope bridge*, which many would come to revere.

Liza was a telegraph operator, as was her husband. They both listened to dots and dashes of Morse code all day long. But their jobs were in jeopardy in 1888, as the telephone was beginning to replace the telegraph. *Who would have a need for their* **soon-to-be-obsolete** *language? They thought.*

Liza thought, *maybe while I stay home with the baby, he can work at another job.*

Jobs were plentiful. The economy of San Angelo was fantastic. The railroad from Ballinger was to be complete in September. Everyone was optimistic that there would be no repeat of the **Panic of 1873** which developed into a depression.

That depression was partly due to large amounts of capital being put into railroads. The same trend was happening in Texas, people worried.

So the mood of the *bridge story* was basically positive. But Liza was not feeling the enthusiasm.

Though Liza was happy to be with child, she harbored a secret that she could not express to her husband. It was with this secret in mind and the laziness of the late June day, that she was forever changed by an event near the *bridge of hope.*

The *hope bridge* had been completed just weeks before the incident. The approaches were still considered dangerous, but they were to be secured soon. This bridge would allow easy passage from San Angelo to Paint Rock and easterly beyond.

On the bank of the Concho River, Liza reflected on someone she loved in Paint Rock. It wasn't her husband, and the irony made her sad.

She was never unfaithful.

And she never planned on being unfaithful. Her platonic love for her husband was good. She would bear his child and hope the baby would change her attitude about deeper love.

Liza retrieved some of her leftover lunch bread while near the bridge. She'd been interpreting code for ten hours. She was exhausted and hungry. She was close to getting home, but just tuckered out. *A short rest by the river would be harmless*, she thought. She sat down, relieved.

So imagine her surprise when, near the dam below the bridge, a lovely mermaid with peachy cheeks emerged from the cool water. Liza rubbed her eyes—as she could not possibly be seeing the imaginary figure.

But the mermaid was really there.

The creature asked if Liza wanted to become her queen. Confused, Liza looked around for support. Finding none, after a lengthy pause she responded with, "I don't know."

The mermaid proceeded to try to entice Liza to come into the water for a celebration of female loveliness. Liza was obviously confused by the request. Bathing in the river was something she'd done many times, but she'd always completed it at night when no one was around.

The mermaid persisted, "Take off your clothes and join me. We can *talk* about love and sacrifice."

Liza, very sweaty, decided to remove her clothes for a quick swim. Being eight months pregnant made overheated her. The cool water would cause no harm, and the mermaid appeared to be friendly.

They swam together and ducked into the water when anyone passed over the bridge. Liza felt better than she had in years. The mermaid was playful and hopeful. Liza's near weightlessness was rewarding, as the burden of the baby's weight that day had taken a toll on her back and hips.

The mermaid shared a secret with Liza, who gasped in amazement. Then she continued to divulge ancient mysteries to Liza as they played in the water. At last, the mermaid asked Liza to share one of *her* confidences.

Liza had had her secret on the tip of her tongue when she heard her husband bawling for her.

He was awakening her from her nap and telling her to go home with him. It was getting late, and they both had to work tomorrow.

"I was so worried about you when I arrived home and you weren't there," he said. "I've been looking for you for thirty minutes."

She was fully clothed and still sweaty. Apparently, she had never gone in the water.

How do you tell your husband that you'd rather live in your dream? That her current life with him was a lie?

That she wanted to cuddle with someone else—a woman?

When my elder told me the Hope Bridge Story, I was skeptical. He concluded saying, "Liza remained faithful to her husband until her dying day."

I thought, *how could she have loved a woman in Paint Rock more than her husband?"*

But that was then, and this is now.

Closets are being emptied as I write.

That story helped me see that gender love is not always what it seems.

I thought, *Somewhere in her dream, Liza had a revelation full of hope.*

Thank goodness in our current society, Liza wouldn't require a dual existence.

And thank goodness a symbol for sexual freedom bridge was erected in 1888.

And her Hope Bridge (Lone Wolf Bridge) still stands.

CHAPTER 19

1888 San Angelo Sisters

Some people are like clouds—when they disappear, it's a brighter day. September 16 of 1888 is the day that Phyllis would always consider her *sunny independence day,* thanks to the bravado of her daughter, Lettie.

Carmen came to live with them after Carmen's husband of twenty years had passed away. It was supposed to be temporary—maybe a few weeks, said Carmen.

Phyllis politely said, "Take as long as you need," but secretly hoped for as short a time as possible.

Guilt about her one-time youthful indiscretion made Phyllis particularly antsy. Phyllis had had her daughter out of wedlock. She'd embarrassed the family horribly. So she and Lettie had been outcasts.

But Carmen and Phyllis had never really gotten along even before that. Carmen was dominant of the children living in a dugout near Ben Ficklin's stage station. And Phyllis wouldn't stand up for herself.

Mama and Papa had reprimanded Carmen for years, but Phyllis was like the runt of the litter.

Lately, however, Phyllis nightly would think of all kinds of comebacks in response to Carmen's offenses of the day. Unfortunately, she normally couldn't think of anything sharp to say at immediate transgressions, until that September 16 in San Angelo. Prior to that day, she'd think of a retort only in the middle of the night.

When Carmen had said, "You run your dress shop shabbily," Phyllis should have responded with, "I'm returning your nose. I found it in my business."

Or when Carmen had said, "Too bad you never married, like I did," Phyllis could have responded, "It doesn't matter who I was, only who I've become."

If only she'd thought of it. Why couldn't she defend herself?

Was Phyllis afraid of change or of losing power struggles?

Phyllis's daughter, Lettie, was stunned at the awkwardness between the two. Lettie, being nineteen, was ever the witty one when Carmen was in a derogatory mood. All three women would be in the dress shop sewing gowns for ladies going to the *Railroad Celebration Ball*, and Carmen would become venomous at the exertion.

Carmen said, "You both should open a smaller shop on Chadbourne Street so that you would pay less rent. Then I wouldn't have to sew."

Lettie countered, "Thanks for your two cents, but I'll give you a quarter to shut up. If anything, we need a larger room for all of the sewing we're doing."

Carmen said, "No work for me. My pretending to listen should be enough for you."

Furious, Lettie responded, "I hope your day is as pleasant as you are."

This kind of back and forth between Lettie and Carmen annoyed Phyllis. She was thankful that Lettie armored herself, though. Phyllis was certain that toxic people, such as Carmen, don't even realize how much they hurt others. Or do they?

Phyllis began to daydream:

—Somewhere in the world smart people were coming up with amazing quotations to address living with a narcissist such as Carmen.

—Somewhere in heaven was the father of her daughter who said he loved both of them, with all his heart.

—Somewhere in the folds of the skirt she was pleating, was the boredom that gave her time to wistfully remember his kisses and passion.

—Somewhere in the past nineteen years she'd hidden her secret from everyone.

—Somewhere in...

The daydream was interrupted.

"I said, 'Every time I sit here, I have a fierce desire to be alone!'" repeated Carmen to Phyllis.

"Prearranged nuptials, hatred of intimacy and lack of children have made me a loner," she added as she scooted her chair away from Lettie and Phyllis. "I much prefer to be back at my ranch in the open air. I don't like being confined to a room with boring work."

"Some people create their own storms and then get upset when it rains," countered Lettie. "If you don't like being here, why don't you just go back to your ranch?"

"How can I expect my sister to raise you properly when she herself got pregnant at the same age that you are currently. I should take you, Lettie, to the ranch. In fact," as if thunderstruck she said, "*we* **will** *go!*"

Lettie said, "I didn't realize you were an expert on my life and how I should live it!"

And so Carmen lectured the two of the advantages of living on a secluded ranch in West Texas.

Phyllis couldn't help but wonder how she would survive without Lettie in her daily life. Phyllis loved Lettie with her whole being. Carmen was certainly never going to take her away—right?

When Carmen made up her mind to take Lettie back to the ranch with her, Phyllis had had enough. Anger heated her core.

Phyllis would have to put Carmen in her place.

Carmen said, "You look as red as a rose, Phyllis. But you know this arrangement would be the best for Lettie."

Finally valor came to Phyllis.

"Since you know it all, you should know when to shut up!" Phyllis raged as she surprised herself with her seriousness.

Carmen shouted, "Your problem is *not knowing* that **you** are the problem!"

"Keep rolling your eyes, you might find a brain back there." Phyllis let her have it.

During the exchange between the sisters, Lettie sat in wonder and admiration of her mother's sudden bout of nerve.

Carmen stood up and said, "They say opposites attract. I hope you meet someone who is good-looking, intelligent, and cultured like my Ray, while I take Lettie to the ranch with me."

Lettie no longer amused, thrashed out of the building in irritation.

Both women were aghast at how they'd been talking about Lettie as if she wasn't even present in the room.

"Ray gave me twenty good platonic years at the ranch. I guess you missed the boat when it came to men. Ray gave me everything except a child. So I'll take yours." Carmen said.

Phyllis finally said what had been on her mind for nineteen years, "Ray also gave me everything I needed."

"What was THAT?" countered Carmen.

"*He gave me Lettie*," shouted Phyllis truthfully and triumphantly.

And THAT was THAT!

CHAPTER 20

1888 The Busy Baker

November 6, 1888

I was in the bakery reading my mom a joke from *Beeton's Book of Jokes and Jests.* "What do you call a giggling bull?"

"I don't know," Mom answered.

A laughingstock—I said, and then I burst out chuckling.

I love jokes, and my Mom likes me to read them to her when my chores are done.

"Have you stacked the wood in the firebox yet?" she asked, while kneading bread dough for the day. "If you have, I have an errand for you. I need baking powder from the General Store."

And that's how the day I got a new dad began.

Until that day, Mom and I'd been drifting from one town to another while she was trying to snag a man. We're both hard workers, but we have a strike against us—we're both *extremely tall* females.

For some reason, men don't want a wife to be a foot taller than they are. I'm only eleven, and I'm as tall as my boss, Joe Akiva, the owner of the bakery.

Speaking of Joe (my new dad), I don't know what he would do without us. One minute he's mixing up dough, and the next minute he's forgotten the dough and is talking to the wood-delivery man. I have to remind him to go back to the dough because, without me, he'd start working on batter for cakes. If there was ever a person with a thousand ideas in his head all at the same time, it would be Mr. Akiva.

He is a stark contrast to Mr. Dressler, who is at the bakery we were at before Joe's. Dressler's Bakery by the Nimitz Hotel is run like a business with a compassionate dictator. We liked working there, but because we're looking for a dad for me, and Mr. Dressler was already married, we got involved with Joe's Bakery on Oakes Street.

But enough about Dressler's. That day, not only did Joe become my dad, but all of the thirty-eight states of America were voting on who would be president of the United States. Incumbent Grover Cleveland was being challenged by Benjamin Harrison.

Because of Election Day, weeks earlier I had an idea to sell promotional presidential cookies with either a "C" or an "H" stamped in the center. We made dozens, upon dozens of the sugar cookies days before the vote. Voting was taking place at the Mays and Wright's office on Concho (which is halfway between Joe's Bakery and Dressler's Bakery.) We knew a lot of people would be out, and we would be ready for them with cookies of their liking.

Then out of the blue, opportunity struck me in the face.

On the way to the General Store, I came upon the preacher talking to a young unmarried couple. They were apparently arranging their nuptials. I stopped to chat with them.

Somewhere in the conversation, I came up with a tactic that might help my mom and me. I then convinced the street-talkers to come to our bakery at six that night for their ceremony. I'd have a wedding cake—free of charge—ready for them.

Throughout the day we were very busy waiting on customers and baking, but I did remember to make a small wedding cake. But, as the day wore on, the Benjamin Harrison campaigners bought all of the "H"-stamped cookies and were luring men on the street, reminding them to vote for Benjamin Harrison.

"And by the way, here is a cookie to prompt you," they'd say.

But back at the bakery we remained busy.

I did find time to ask my mom, "Have you ever just flat-out asked a man to marry you?"

"Are you kidding?" she replied with a quizzical look on her face. And that was the end of that. I thought.

So, I'd have to rely on my scheme to get a dad.

I went to Joe and asked, "Have you ever thought about marrying my mom?" This became thought number twenty-seven of the fifty thoughts concurrently running through his mind.

He smilingly replied, "I'll think about it," then went about the shop crazy-eyed.

My spirits were lifted. Later, I told him that I'd watch the bakery because he had forgotten to vote, and here it was nearly 5:30!

While he was gone, I told my mom, "Joe is thinking about marrying you."

She turned beet red and claimed that I was in big trouble for meddling in her business.

"Mom, it's my life, too," I said over the noise of the flurry of people coming into the bakery.

At six o'clock there were lots of people packed in the small shop for the wedding. *Gosh, I hope I made a big enough cake*, I thought.

Joe came back to the bakery and was dumbfounded by the crowd. I explained the deal I'd made with the preacher and the couple to him.

His brain was overflowing with confusion. Thought number twenty-seven (he marries my mom) had already vacated his brain's vault. But I reminded him that he'd said there was a possibility—

And so without much more commotion, one wedding became a double wedding—as I had planned—and the joke was on my mom. The guests ate the wedding cake, while Joe, Mom, and I ate the leftover cookies stamped with the "C."

Later that night, when Mom and I moved into the upstairs area of the bakery with Joe, I told them I'd sleep downstairs. I then asked, "Are y'all mad at me?"

Joe said, "I'm glad I have a wife and business partner. I got a good deal today."

Mom said to me, "You grabbed the bull by its horns."

"And now I'll take the man at his word," she said as she bent down to give Joe a whopping big kiss.

We won, I thought.

Weeks later I found out that Benjamin Harrison had—surprisingly—won the presidency.

My cookie craftiness had done the trick with that quandary as well.

CHAPTER 21

1888 The Clock

Margie was desperate to have both of her clocks chime at the same time. *And they should be in synch with the courthouse clock as well*, she thought. It wasn't so much to ask her husband, Floyd, to faithfully wind the clocks at the exact same time every week so the resulting chiming would be uninterrupted. But he didn't see the importance of it.

He thought she was unreasonable and had an unhealthy zeal towards keeping perfect time.

Of course, he would always be prompt at receiving his meals and going to bed, though. She had him trained.

One day she found on her doorstep a box of straw. Buried in the straw were a note and a clock. Margie's first thought was, *Would it keep good time with her current clocks?* She did not even look at the note until her husband came home from work. She assumed that her good husband had given her the timepiece—he knew of her passion for perfect time.

At her husband's prompt arrival at six o'clock, she thanked him for the gift. But since he knew nothing of the present, he investigated the box and the note. The note said, *Meet me at the courthouse at seven o'clock, and I will tell you about the magic of this valuable clock.* **Whatever you do, don't wind it until we talk!**

Now, Margie and Floyd had simple habits each weekday evening. Supper was precisely at six o'clock. At seven, Floyd would smoke his pipe and read, while Margie crocheted. At eight, they would take their dog for a walk until nine. Then it would be time for bed.

Saturday nights afforded a bath in the kitchen instead of the walk.

So the implication that one or both of them should walk to the courthouse by seven, put a rush on their supper and a damper on their ordinary routine.

"But we must go to the courthouse to find out about this device! What if it is vexed? We could return it," said Floyd.

"Certainly it is mysterious, but I don't want to upset our ordinary routine," she answered.

"Oh, you and your traditions! We live such uniform lives that I can practically predict when I will sneeze and when you will fart," he countered. "If we hurry we can take the clock with us in a wheelbarrow and walk our dog at the same time."

"I guess this will be acceptable for this one time. We don't want to depend on careless alternatives to our pattern of living. Nothing is more important than continuity," she replied.

And so it was. Their dog was surprised that he was being walked early. He knew when the clocks chimed eight that he should grab his collar and leash. Walking at 6:30 p.m. was unheard of in the Fritch residence.

At the specified time and place, the couple arrived to see a strange-looking man in a yellow slicker. There was no rain, so the slicker seemed out of place. Also, there was a bulge under the yellow coat that worried Margie, so she addressed the man with a voice of authority.

"Sir, you will not have a gun under your slicker. Drop it, or we will dump this clock out of the wheelbarrow immediately," she ordered.

He quietly removed what was bulging from the slicker to show them an extremely large key. "I have no gun on me. I'm unarmed except for the message that will change your lives forever."

The couple lost their innate fear of the stranger when he continued to talk. "I possess this key to that magical clock you found on your doorstep today. The key inserts into the back and can be turned to the right to unlock *prompt traditions* in your life."

Margie stated, "Sir, I think that clock is something I could use. There is nothing as comforting as repetitive tendencies in my life."

Floyd didn't see the magic as something he would embrace. You see, Floyd was quite bored with the uniformity of his life. He'd thought of visiting saloons as a means of diversion in his practically *scripted* life.

"I don't want this clock and its magic. Take it back and leave my wife and me alone," Floyd said.

The man was compelled to list one concern of the perfect-timing clock. "If you choose to use this key, you will certainly have a set routine in life. But on the contrary, somewhere, *one person on earth will be forever* **tardy to affairs**," ended the man.

"Who would it be?" asked Margie, genuinely concerned.

"It could be someone you know or a perfect stranger from somewhere else in these thirty-eight states of America." With that, he threw the key into the wheelbarrow and left.

Floyd wanted to dump the items and go to a saloon for a drink.

But Margie pushed the wheelbarrow herself and chatted, "It is a perfectly good clock that will look great above the mantle in our bedroom. We don't have to use the key to *wake the magic*. Let's just take it home."

So they did. She would use the key eventually, she thought.

Over time, she became antsy about the key and its magic.

There were plenty of stragglers in life already.

What would one more matter?

But for days they argued about the clock.

Finally one day she inserted the key as the man had said. Half an hour later at 6 p.m. her three clocks rang exactly as the courthouse clock chimed. She was elated.

Then Floyd did not come home for supper at six as he had for years. He was VERY tardy.

She found his *I'm-leaving-you* note by the dog's leash.

She decided she would miss his tardiness from her life.

Yes, she would miss him but was still delighted with her perfectly timed clocks.

Floyd left her boring lifestyle.

She lived in that same house, listening to her three clocks chime perfectly in unison with the courthouse clock, for forty-three years.

When the courthouse clock was stolen in 1929, she died and was forever known as *that strange 'time crazy' woman.*

CHAPTER 22

1889 Face It

Due to his strict Catholic upbringing, he had tithed his entire life. Anna, his wife, said, "We can't afford to give to the church right now. Our income is so low we can barely make ends meet."

John replied, "You must exhale in order to inhale. God will provide to those who give cheerfully."

They were analyzing their budget at the kitchen table in their humble dairy home. Mason jars for their milk earnings were sorted into categories of their expenses. The church jar had coins in it that Anna thought they needed elsewhere.

Laura, their five-year-old, was by the cast-iron stove, playing with her doll. Some would say that John and Anna were having a healthy discussion of their finances—others might say they were arguing.

Times were actually booming for most commerce in San Angelo. The year was 1889, and this county seat was bustling with a new railroad station, multitudes of businesses, and an ice factory. It was the availability of ice that had brought John and Anna to the West Texas town in the first place.

If you want to sell something that could be refrigerated, you want customers with access to ice.

But they weren't the only people who wanted to capitalize on dairy products in the city; there was a lot of competition.

The family worked hard at their six-cow dairy on Donkey Flats.

Prior to the 1880s, most families used their own cow's daily milk for butter, cheese, and children—not necessarily in that order. Ice cream was unknown in the Concho Valley unless there was a hailstorm. Butter was made with a churn; milk for cheese was curdled with acid and rennin. The rennin for cheese-making was derived from the fourth stomach of unwanted veal—male younglings who, obviously, couldn't produce milk. Without refrigeration, milk was allowed to clabber for a *different tasting* product. Families with a cow could get adequate dairy products without 'buying' them.

But commercial dairies were becoming more prevalent when Texas urbanization occurred in the prairie. John and Anna were trying to have a profitable dairy of their own.

Dairies only need one male for the herd to be successful. The more precious feed going to the females—the more the milk revenue. And milk cows require lots of water and should have good genetics.

"If you can buy a Jersey male, your new cows born of his seed will produce more butterfat," Anna had read.

"Oh, I don't think there's a market for country butter anymore. Oleomargarine is beginning to be used more often because of its convenience," he countered. "Maybe we should sell off our herd and buy milk from other dairies for cheese making. We could be exclusively cheese mongers."

That didn't sit well with Anna.

They just couldn't agree. But they mostly didn't compromise on the ten percent offering to the church. They just discussed their options further every few weeks.

There was a problem.

The community had attracted several small dairies at about the same time that John and Anna had arrived. With the supply for milk greater than the demand, John and Anna were struggling.

Their small tract of land near Kirby's place on the north side of town was ideal for their dairy. It also had all the amenities that Anna wanted for the large family she was hoping for.

But the low prices for the milk products did not meet the great expenses of good-quality supplements, feed, and the water well.

Mr. Titus had drilled for water and found it at ninety feet. He placed a windmill over the underground pump and sent John the bill. If you think no one cares if you're dead or alive, try missing a few payments. Mr. Titus knows where John lives, to be sure. Hopefully, John will have that loan paid off in a few months.

Besides consumable expenses, capital improvements, and land payments, there would always be taxes. So another jar at the kitchen table was for the taxes that must be paid to Tom Green County. "We should strangle anyone who thinks that the county tax rate is fair," says Anna frequently. Somehow, they've managed to cough up the currency when the sheriff came to call. But it was hard.

One way that John cut family costs was to boycott any establishment that sells items he cannot afford. Consequently he shopped at only a few of the stores in town.

He and Anna were frugal. They cut each other's hair. Anna made their clothing and bedding. John troubleshooted all household difficulties. Presents from family in East Texas always seemed to come at the direst time in the money cycle. John and Anna sometimes wondered if they should just pack up and head back to the home folks in Moravia. But there were difficulties at hand, there, as well.

One way Anna tried to make ends meet was by creating different flavors of cheese to sell. She also was combining different herbs and spices together in a separate, secret project—a scheme that only she and Laura knew about.

For the cheeses and milk, John rigged up an evaporative cooling room with the well water. He used some old drapes and a rejected steam pump—that he brought back to life with new gaskets and rings.

That spring-house room was adequate for the aging cheeses and to cool the milk they'd bring into town to sell. The girls were very proud of him, because without cooling they would have to let the milk clabber. There was less money brought in for clabbered milk versus fresh, sweet milk.

After John got the cooling system going, his next mission was to cull the small herd into a fantastic gene pool. He agreed with Anna that a Jersey bull would be a great asset to the operation, but they just didn't have the money for one, yet.

Meanwhile, Laura had gotten attached to a male calf that needed to be slaughtered. She wanted Star (named so because of the head's fur disfigurement) to be the next family bull. But Leroy (the family's current bull) was still doing his job of impregnating the females, just fine.

Star was a cutie, following Laura around. Laura had been Star's mother—bottle feeding him since he was three days old. John had a difficult time convincing Laura that Star should become veal, and his stomach should provide rennin for Anna's cheeses. She cried when she learned of Star's destiny.

"Oh, put your tears on simmer," John had said as he lovingly consoled her. He didn't know how he was going to explain that Star was going to disappear from their lives soon.

Oh, why couldn't Laura have been a boy? he regularly thought.

The midwife had come into the kitchen holding a girl the day that Anna went into labor five years ago. That day had been something of a disappointment to John—happy and yet sad.

Ironically, when John helped his cows give birth, he'd be so very delighted when the calf arrived female. He'd whistle a unique song, knowing that he wouldn't have to cull this calf from the herd.

But having human girls in the family was different.

If I can't have a boy, at least I can have a tomboy, he thought.

Laura was not a tomboy, as John had repeatedly wished. Laura played with girl toys. Laura liked to read. Laura had learned to read already, due to her mother's obsessive desire to read newspapers, books, and even labels.

From East Texas one Christmas, a book of jokes that Anna and Laura were compelled to try on John, arrived. Laura memorized the book. It was then that John realized elephants and children never forget. And they like to repeat and repeat and repeat.

Two jokes from the book—A farmer is asked how long cows should be milked. The farmer replies, "The same as short ones." John thought it was hilarious when Laura pulled that one on him the *first* time.

Anna countered the joke with another: "A farmer's wife was asked, 'Is it easy to milk a cow?'"

Anna replied, "Sure. Any jerk can do it!"

But being in agriculture wasn't all fun and games. A dairy man had a lot of decisions to make for his herd and his family. If the rain was sufficient, then the herd could feed on the acreage without too much supplemental food.

But the milk would have to be weekly analyzed for the quality and quantity of cream that floated to the top. Butter from cream was a better seller, compared to the more perishable milk. Healthier food for the cows cost money he didn't have. Lesser-quality food meant slighter-valued milk and cream.

And sometimes the cows became stressed from the weather or wolf threats. These could cause them to produce less milk. He had his cows on a schedule: when they were impregnated, when they would give birth, when they would give milk, and when the cycle would start all over again. He tried to have a constant quantity of milk each day. There was a lot of planning and luck when it came to managing a herd for milk.

Feeding animals that couldn't bring a profit was something he always thought about when he and Anna would stare at the Mason jars on the table. There was always tension between John and Anna when they discussed finances. But there was also an unspoken clash between them.

Why hasn't Anna gotten pregnant again? John wondered. They had planned on having a big family as their ancestors had. Infant mortality was still horribly high during this decade, but Anna had only gotten pregnant one time in six years. That was ridiculous in John's mind. It wasn't his fault, he knew. *What is the problem?* he'd ask himself.

John was always thinking like a farmer. He'd hint to Anna, "Are you eating enough? Are you staying stress-free? Are you overworked?"

Anna would be disappointed each month when her period signaled yet another mismatch of sperm and egg. Her sisters and friends in Moravia were having children, galore. Sometimes she wondered if loneliness was the cause of the problem.

She missed her parents and siblings in East Texas. She had written many a time for them to come to San Angelo for a visit, or to settle. The words had fallen on deaf ears, it seemed. So Anna bought spices and herbs to satisfy her unease. These were costs that John thought unnecessary.

"You can't buy happiness, but it sure makes misery easier to live with," alleged Anna one night months later, when they were again looking at the jars.

Agriculture is the only occupation where all the risk lies with the producer, but he only gets a small piece of the pie. Then that piece has to pay for all of their expenses.

Uncertainty of income was their biggest concern because of competing dairies.

Uncertainty of everything (except God's love) could creep into their thoughts if they let it. Fortunately they had a church to go to every

Sunday. Even though the Mass was in Latin, and there was mostly the priest's backside to look at, the sermons in English seemed to give direction for them. Their Bible at home also gave them comfort when they read the New Testament daily before bedtime.

Anna asked John where in the Bible tithing is mentioned, as she did not want to do it. John scrambled to find it, but quoted, "In the book of Numbers, chapter eighteen."

These verses did not remedy her curiosity or trust. Every night they brought out the Bible. Every night the book's center pages reminded her of their marriage date, Laura's birth and baptism dates, and the blank lines for additional children she seemed incapable of having.

Twice weekly, they made love. *Why on earth aren't I pregnant?* she thought.

To divert her attention from children, she would shop when she went to town. The tithing hadn't brought them more children, so the tithing portion of their earnings she would spend on spices occasionally.

Sometimes John rebuked her. She claimed they were bargains. He explained while massaging her shoulders once, "A bargain is something you don't need at a price you can't resist!"

One Saturday he pointed to an ad in the *San Angelo Standard Times.* "Anna, did you notice that the paprika you bought last week went on sale today?" She fumed in response. "Isn't that how it always is?"

But John loved Anna and Laura, as evidenced by all of his hard work for them. He milked the cows twice a day. He cleaned the milk buckets and the cans with ashes afterward. He delivered the skim milk to the few clients he had. He also sold butter, eggs, cream, and cheese to people in town. He fed the calves bottles, (except for Star) until they were ready to be either slaughtered or weaned. He tinkered with the windmill and his used steam pump to make them more efficient. And he kept the cows out of the garden, where Ann's vegetables, herbs, and flowers gave her so much comfort.

Yes, John and Anna were like two peas in a pod, in love with similar goals. Laura was the pea plant's tendril grasping at the universe. What more would the family require?

"Anna, all you really need is food, shelter, and compliments," teased John every day. He provided all—the best that he could.

But he had another longing, besides the large family of sons he'd dreamt about. You see, John's Dad's dying wish was that he would continue working with cows, as his ancestors had.

This haunted John. John liked working with cattle, but the perishable milk products were inharmonious with his psyche. He had always wanted to work with cows, but he longed to be a *butcher*.

He should have been more specific with God all these years of praying, it seems. The idea of being a dairyman had been imprinted in his brain, as this is what the Gloutz family had always done. How could he be different?

"I thought I wanted a dairy. Turns out I just wanted cows and the money they make. I like butchering cows when they are past their prime of making milk."

He continued to tell Laura how much he enjoyed making sausage out of the less desirable meat scraps. She loved eating the links straight out of the smokehouse. He was good at what he did.

"Let's get out of the dairy business gradually," Anna heard John say one evening as he was placing coins in the Mason jars.

She was shocked but intrigued at the notion.

"What would we do? Stay here or move back to the Hill Country?" she inquired.

"Anna, what do you think of selling the land and the dairy and moving into San Angelo. You make a terrific barbeque rub for beef and chicken with your blends of spices and herbs," he replied.

"You like my blends?" she was surprised, as she wasn't aware that he even knew about them.

"You have a real talent!" he said as he pulled her up from the chair to dance. "We can start a meat business instead of the milk trade."

"You are insane!" she replied smilingly, as he twirled her around the kitchen.

Laura thought they were both foolish, but was glad they were so happy.

"I've tasted your secret stashes in jars throughout the kitchen." Each jar had a recipe strung to it. "Anna, you've mastered seasoning beef."

"We could cater weddings and funerals! We could start a butcher club in town and spice the meat for them at a reasonable price. They won't be able to resist," Anna responded.

Laura chimed in, "And Star could be my pet bull."

The festivities came to a standstill.

"I tell you what, Laura—if he turns out to be an even-tempered bull with good descendants, we'll barter him out as a servicing stud," he said as he picked her up to dance as a trio.

"Let's have barbeque for breakfast," Anna said gleefully.

And two days later, they did!

CHAPTER 23

1889 Guarding the Plate

"Guard the plate!" someone from the group of onlookers shouted. Only moments before, Erwin—on third base—suspected that the next hit would be a bunt to first. It was the top of the ninth inning, two outs, full count on the batter, and Erwin's run would mean a lot. No pressure to be a fast runner, for which Erwin had flair. Whether feeling pressured all of the time or running reckless some of the time, Erwin had talent for both.

Erwin was like many males in West Texas—young, thin, and eager. He actually lived near Coleman at an open coal-deposit mine. By train he got to San Angelo the previous day with his Brownwood baseball buddies. Most of his teammates were going back to Brownwood the next day, but Erwin wanted to stay in town for another day to visit his sister, Maggie. Erwin surprised Maggie when he took up mining for income. She was amazed when he started playing baseball for leisure. He'd been as haphazard as the wind for most of his life.

That's because he was just an indecisive kind of guy. He and his sister had been orphaned in Minnesota in 1865 and, willy-nilly, had become part of a growing Texas. They'd been raised by their grandma in Austin, Texas. Both in their 20s now, they'd aged quickly when grandma died. That's about the time that Erwin began shifting from job to job and starting to play baseball. Day to day, Erwin said to himself, *I just want a fresh start*.

But back to the present game, he was determined to break the tie for his team, especially since Claud was such a jerk.

Claud had beaned him on his second pitch for a walk. Claud was an aggressive pitcher, and it seemed like he had it in for *Home-Run Erwin*. But Erwin was prone to taking things personally. He'd made it to third base, and, by golly, he was gonna keep going even if he had to steal home plate.

"That was a perfect bunt!" said someone in the crowd at the crack of a bat.

So from third, he found the catcher blocking the plate. Erwin plowed into Pete and was the hero until the next batter punched a home run. Then, as hoped for, the Brownwood pitcher struck out the San Angeloans three times. The Brownwood guys won the game, and Erwin was especially happy to sneer at Claud and Pete. Many of the guys went to the nearby saloon to celebrate, but not Erwin.

After the game, Erwin went to Maggie's hut for supper. She'd been widowed a year and was supporting her two kids by being a seamstress. She was nice most of the time, except when she scolded Erwin for being wishy-washy. He sent her most of his paycheck since his brother-in-law's passing. *Why wasn't she appreciative?* he thought.

Being at her home was really about chopping wood and making repairs. The children bothered him, since his patience was as sparse as a bird's brain. *Was I this bad when I was little?* he wondered.

If he'd been a better man, he would have stayed at Maggie's longer. But the incessant crying and yelling lured him to the train earlier than originally planned. As he walked down Chadbourne to the train station, he considered how he and Maggie had roughed it—yet had also been pampered by their grandma. She taught them to read and work hard. The *working hard* part had not planted in Erwin, though. He had been quite shiftless—until the mining job surfaced.

What kept him at the coal mines was the secure pay. Many people were changing from wood-burning to coal-burning in their houses—so coal was becoming very popular. Since Maggie was a widow, he had an incentive to stick with one good job. The coal-loading job was alright, but his boss was tip-top. The foreman understood how important baseball was to him and let him go into Brownwood occasionally for practices and games. His boss even encouraged Erwin to go to San Angelo to play, since he knew of Maggie's husband's demise.

Getting closer to the train station, he had a nagging thought. He'd given Maggie his last coin and was in a quandary as to how he would pay for his train ticket. *I'll just sneak into an empty cattle car*, he thought, as he passed a hat shop.

"Say, are you going to the train station?" the owner of the store asked. She was holding a sizeable crate at her doorway.

"Yea, I'm on my way to Coleman County," Erwin replied. "What do you need?"

"This package needs to go to Ballinger, and I'm busy to where I can't walk it over to the train myself. I thought if you were going, being all strong and everything, that you could do it."

Erwin noticed that she was pretty and possibly single. "Sure I can. Do you think I'm honest?"

She blushed, "I don't know what a man would do with these lady's hats—unless you plan to sell them yourself—but yes, I trust you."

They made their introductions, and she gave him the box and its fare. Waving with gratitude, she then returned to her shop, where three customers were waiting.

Erwin carried the box. It would have been so much easier if he'd had a horse and wagon. *Oh well, it's just two more blocks.* And by walking, he'd had the chance to meet a possibly eligible female.

I might be coming to San Angelo more often if she's available, he thought to himself, as he neared the train.. He noticed the engineer was finishing his coffee as coal and water were being loaded. He'd never contributed a parcel to the freight part of the train. But without too much difficulty he secured his future girlfriend's package for Ballinger. And then he found himself sorely tempted to sneak into the freight car—where the hats had gone—for a free ride.

But someone interrupted his thought.

"Hey, you! I've seen you at the coal mine. What are you doing in Angelo?" asked the man tending the firebox.

"I play baseball for the Brownwood team," he answered.

"Are you going back today? I'm thinking you are just the man I need for a favor," replied the fire keeper.

Erwin asked, "What do you mean?"

"Well, you've seen the new safety bicycles around, right? I have a crate in the freight car with an unassembled one. I need *you* to shovel coal into the firebox in my stead, so I can put the bike together for my ride home within Brownwood."

Erwin replied, "How about I construct your bike for you instead? I shovel coal all day at my job. I'd rather not do it now!"

But the guy wouldn't let up. "Look, I shovel about forty pounds per mile, and Ballinger is only thirty-six miles away. Just think of the baseball workout you would get! You do it, and I put together the bike. My engineer says it's OK."

"Look, I need a ride to Coleman County, but I just don't want to do any shoveling. I can put that bike into shape for you, though."

So it was decided that Erwin would get the bicycle done. He hopped into the boxcar with a few tools that the fireman had given him.

In that freight car, who do you think might have been sitting there but Claud and Pete?

"What are you guys doing here?" asked Erwin.

"We're tired of mucking out the horse droppings at the stables in Angelo, so we're leaving to look for other work," barked Claud. "What are the odds of us sharing a boxcar, huh?"

Erwin saw the open crate with the bike parts and sighed. Now, not only would he have to figure out how to assemble it, but apparently, he would have an audience of jerks, while he was at it.

"Why aren't y'all in the passenger car?" Erwin asked.

"Filled up, so we got a discount to travel in here. You must have gotten the discount, too," said Pete.

"Yep, in a manner of speaking," was Erwin's reply.

The train began to inch its way to Miles, Rowena, and Ballinger, while Erwin explained his deal with the fireman and the bike. It was awkward using train tools too large for the intricate bolts. The vibrations didn't help either. For a while, Pete held the bike steady, while Erwin examined the picture's details. It turned out that Erwin and Pete shared a commonality. Both were catchers most of the time, so they talked while Erwin worked. They weren't enemies as he'd felt during yesterday's game.

"Fort Concho is an interesting place," remarked Erwin.

"Yea. We like playing there because it's not as dusty as some of the other places in town," explained Pete. "We are getting to be a better team than we were in April. Gosh, we were horrible in the spring. All along, though, Claud is our greatest asset!"

"Well, practice a lot and play tough opponents, and y'all will get better and better," said Erwin.

Later during the trip to Coleman County, Claud was snoozing while he leaned against a crate. His violin was by his side. You'd never have thought, from his peaceful sleep posture, that he was the one who had beaned Erwin the day before. Erwin's left arm was still bruised and throbbing from that incident. And he hadn't forgiven him of the bad pitch, either. Had he been thrown a good ball, he'd no doubt have hit a home run. But there Claud was, hat over eyes, snoring.

After a big bump in the track, the violin went sliding toward the open door. When Erwin grabbed it, he nearly dropped it as he heard the familiar rattlesnake caution noise.

"What the heck?" exclaimed Erwin.

"What are you doing with my fiddle?" asked the now-awake Claud.

Pete replied, "He just saved your fiddle for you, you fool. It had almost shattered into the ground!"

"Is there a rattlesnake in there? Heavens, I nearly wet my pants grabbing that," said Erwin, as he quickly handed it to Claud.

"It's just the rattle from a snake I killed in Irion County last May. You know what they say, it's a good luck charm to keep other rattlers away," he replied as he handled the fiddle.

Claud then continued to talk about ranching, politics, and women for the rest of the journey.

There was an unusual silence briefly while the train was slowing down in Ballinger. Erwin was on his knees, looking for the last nut to go on the bike. Nowhere to be seen, it had gone into the corner of the car during the bump. Unbeknownst to the three guys, the nut was directly next to a poisonous spider, which had hitched a ride with a crate.

"I am so frustrated because I know that nut is somewhere in this boxcar. I counted all of them before I got started, so it's either still in here amongst these crates, or it fell through the door when I was catching the fiddle," lamented Erwin.

"We'll help look for it," said Pete. And he lightly punched Claud in the shoulder. All three men were on hands and knees, moving crates around. Finally Claud saw the silver nut, but he also saw a spider the size of a large button. He wasn't scared of rattlesnakes, but a spider sent him into panic. He moved away so quickly that he almost pushed the other guys out of the open door. The train hadn't stopped yet, so everyone was a bit flustered and confused.

"I can't be in the same car as that spider," he said, as he pointed to the spider and the nut. He jumped out of the slowing train nearing the depot.

With laughing eyes, Pete stepped on the spider and retrieved the nut. Erwin finished the bike. The rest of the journey turned out to be easy. For that leg of the trip it was Pete, Erwin, and the fireman in the freight car.

Claud had talked the fireman into shoveling coal, since he was certain that the boxcar held the entire family of the brown recluse spiders.

As the train neared the mining camp, Erwin jumped off and walked a bit to his tent. *I just want a fresh start*, he thought. With that, his mind drifted to a certain girl at a hat shop. He'd been so nervous when they introduced themselves that he had forgotten her name—something with a "G?" He went to sleep thinking of her. He'd nickname her "Beauty" until her name came back to him.

What happened the next day was so ridiculous that the confrontation got the attention of the whole camp. Erwin woke up to hear a fiddle playing, and out of curiosity he followed the sound to—whom else—but Claud and Pete. Those two had gotten off the train near the camp and had probably walked parallel to Erwin in the brush in the dark. Even though there'd been a full moon, Erwin didn't see them get to camp and ask the foreman for jobs. Thank goodness they would be on the picking crew instead of the shoveling crew—as Erwin was.

"What are you guys doing here?" Erwin shouted over the fiddle song.

"We told you that we didn't want do stable work anymore. Coal doesn't stink like manure does. We're gonna give this a try. We're even going to play baseball on your team, if they'll have us," Pete replied.

This is not good, thought Erwin. *First of all, the team already has a catcher—me, and second of all, I don't want to be the catcher when*

Claud is the pitcher. He knew he could work with cantankerous fellows—God knows there were several odd ducks already working at the mine. *But my recreation time shouldn't include that jerk, Claud,* was his conclusion.

A week passed by slowly, as the miners did their jobs and got to know each other. Claud continued to be stern, crusty, and surly. Pete was OK. In fact after supper one night, Pete pulled Erwin aside and showed him a box of odds and ends for his little sister. There were blue and red feathers from local wild birds. Buttons, chains, and broken jewelry were in there, too. But the strangest items in the box were rattles from the snake with the same name.

"What are all of these pieces for?" asked Erwin.

Pete replied, "I collect these for Trudy, so she can sew them as decorations into ladies' things. I'm showing you this because I'd be honored for you to come with me tomorrow during lunch to look for more stuff. I think I saw an albino turkey out in the brush, and I think Trudy would like some of its feathers."

"Well, I'm good with that. It beats the boredom of camp for sure," said Erwin.

"Great. We'll make it a plan. And I saw your ball and glove in the train, so maybe we can practice a bit out here," said Pete.

Erwin considered having Pete as a friend and liked it—so it was. They hunted for sewable, colorful nature objects and even killed a few rattlesnakes for the rattles. They played catch, and Pete began to coach Erwin on becoming a pitcher. They moved coal and ate meals with the crew and found that they had a lot in common during their time off.

Claud, on the other hand, was like some of the other peculiars in the camp, always moody. He could chatter your ear off about anything, and when you got tired of his talking, he'd play music loudly.

If Claud caught you for a minute, you would be trapped with him until the foreman let you go back to work. Erwin avoided Claud at all costs. There was just something about the guy that made them incompatible.

Concho Folks

Then an unavoidable trip occurred. Only Claud, Pete, and Erwin went to Brownwood one day to get some horses reshod at the blacksmith shop. They timed the trip so that they were also in town for a game against the Brady team. The Brownwood team had accepted Claud and Pete a few weeks earlier at practice. During the game, Pete and Erwin switched off as catcher and right field. Claud and the original pitcher switched off, as well. One good thing about Claud was that he was a good pitcher. Brownwood beat Brady. Everybody got along for the game.

But that night, another type of game was played by a few members of the team. That game was straight poker, and it did not end well at all. The game was terrorized by Claud because he was prone to shorting the pot, slipping in concealed cards, or double dealing to himself. Every time he won the pot, the others would almost catch him in the act of cheating—but not quite! Arguments ensued with each showdown in which Claud won the pot. He knew how to cheat inconspicuously.

Back at camp one night, a poker game was assembling. If Claud was playing, Erwin would not. Gradually the other miners were catching on that when Claud played cards it was like tossing your money into a wishing well without getting your wish. To be as stupid as to play poker with Claud was to be as dumb as a doornail. But you couldn't warn the new recruits fast enough. Newbies yearned for the excitement of saloons, which the mining camp didn't have.

Anyway, the card game began with a new deck that the foreman bought in Brownwood. At least the cards weren't marked, and there were no extra ones. Erwin and Pete were in a tent next to the card-game tent. They planned to laugh while eavesdropping on the rookies next door—getting their dose of fraud. But that's where Erwin and Pete were wrong, about thirty minutes into the game.

"Poker is one hundred percent skill and fifty percent luck," Claud's voice boomed. He'd been drinking.

131

"I'm in," says another. "I fold," says yet another.

Boom went a gun as players ran out of the tent. Claud had put a hole in the card tent for no particular reason. He'd never done anything like that before as far as anyone knew. But the bullet had made its way into the tent next door—straight into and out Erwin's left shoulder.

"What the heck!" exclaimed Erwin, as his right hand grabbed the bullet hole. Everyone was hunkering low until the foreman proved that Claud was no longer armed. It took a while for everyone to get over the excitement.

Because of this incident, no one was allowed to have any cards in the mining camp anymore. Claud had ruined it for everyone. It was something that would bother Erwin until the end of time.

Weeks passed, and things settled down some in the camp. The minor shoulder wound healed nicely, but playing baseball wasn't happening for Erwin. He'd had a *fresh start* without wanting one.

And since he couldn't shovel coal for a while, he became assistant cook—peeling potatoes and onions. He also went out into the brush looking for deer for stew. He tended to the horses and helped the foreman with anything that didn't require a good left shoulder.

You don't realize how much you need a shoulder until you've lost it, he thought. *That blasted Claud!* The foreman had to keep them separated. Claud would have been fired, but the boss loved the fiddling and so kept him on.

Being a bit on the mend, Erwin asked if he could go back to San Angelo to bring Maggie some money for the kids. He also thought his gunshot wound could earn him sympathy points with his Beauty. His wish was granted, and so he walked to the track, and the fireman of the train let him ride with the engineer to Ballinger.

Meanwhile in Ballinger, four boxcars of circus and carnival people and their equipment were being added to the train in route for Angelo. This was Erwin's lucky day. He figured he could take Maggie and the two brats to the celebration and have a great time forgetting about Claud and the bullet. Maybe he'd see his Beauty there as a bonus!

Maggie and the kids were excited, as was the rest of the town. Two huge tents were set up, one for the circus and the other for the sideshows.

Going to the fair was like a breath of fresh air. Instead of dark coal smudges, there were bright, clean colors, noise, and spectacle. First the little family went to the sideshows, where they saw a bearded woman, a four-legged, two-armed boy, and a man with hooved hands and feet. There were also some jars. One held a two-headed snake, another a four-footed chicken. The last contained a mermaid.

The fair included some vendors selling tamales and ice cream. Ah! The smell made everyone hungry. The place was brimming with gasping, laughing, and eating. The marvelous tradition of circus and carnival was peppered with skill, danger, magic, and thrills. The good-natured crowd was a blessing for Erwin, who was used to Claud tension in Coleman County.

Everything was going so well that afternoon. Then it got even better with a brief glimpse of Beauty—out with some girls. The group of ladies was having fun just as the little family was. Erwin *was not seen* by Beauty, since there was so much going on, but he sure did set his eyes on her.

It occurred to him that Beauty might mistake his sister for a girlfriend, so he became standoffish to Maggie and the kids—in case she looked his way. He just couldn't remember her name—"G" for Gwendolyn? Gigi? Grace? Oh, why couldn't he remember?

It was time for the show to begin, so everyone walked into the big top. Erwin could see Beauty, but she could not see him. The first act was a unicycler who also juggled. The stilt walkers came next, as the contortionists were preparing for their act. The bed of nails seemed impossible to lie on, but the half-naked man showed how it could be done. This traveling circus had plenty of thrills.

The animals consisted of two monkeys, a Mexican black bear, and some cute dogs which could dance their way into your heart. All along the fun was getting more explosive. Soon the fire swallower entered the ring. Oohs and aahs continued. Clowns were a nuisance but were need-ed during the changing of acts.

By and by, the final act of plate spinning was about to start. Mr. Spin-ner told some clean *plate jokes*, as the audience helped him remem-ber that he needed to rev up the spin on certain plates while he joked around. Mr. Spinner had six plates spinning on sticks on the table. He had them numbered.

"What's the big difference between a plate and a bugger?" asked Mr. Spinner.

"One's on top of the table, and the other is under the table," he joked.

Everyone laughed at this and all of his jokes. The tension of remind-ing him to spin certain plates was hilarious.

Bang! There was a loud noise at the entrance of the tent, and all of the sudden Claud on a horse entered the big top.

Is this part of the act? People wondered.

"I'm going to shoot each of those dang plates. And then y'all are all going straight home." Claud announced.

Then, sure as his word, he shot five of the six plates with accuracy a pitcher would have. When he was reloading, Erwin dove into the ring to guard plate six from Claud. Erwin saved the plate but got struck by a bullet in his left shoulder—again. The plate was reminiscent of his grandma's set, and he just couldn't let the pattern be destroyed.

Now the place was in chaos, as some bystanders apprehended Claud and confiscated his gun. But something magical happened while that was going on. Beauty was next to Erwin and had put his head in her lap. He was about to go into shock, when she said, "Do you remember me from the hat shop?"

He closed his eyes and let out, "Yes. But I don't remember your name."

"It's Trudy, and I'm going to help you get through this. You look like you need a *fresh start*."

CHAPTER 24

1889 Jumping to Conclusions

"This is the last time I'll be here at church with you, Sister," said Bonnie, as she blessed herself with holy water. "Wallace is coming Friday and taking me home Saturday," she added.

The Latin Mass at Immaculate Conception Church had been cool and comfortable. The homily had stressed Proverbs 19:21—"You can make many plans, but the Lord's purpose will prevail."

"I really needed to hear the sermon today because none of my plans have been panning out lately," she continued, as she loosened her tight belt. She also unfastened the button at her waist.

Bonnie and her sister, Jenny, had been living together in San Angelo for about four months. Bonnie had wintered there with Jenny. Both women were in their twenties and well cared for.

"Special delivery for Bonnie Fife," shouted the telegram delivery boy. Bonnie removed a tip from her purse and received three folded, numbered messages.

Bonnie questioned, "Why are these numbered?"

"I don't know," replied the lad, "but you are only to open the first one now, and it will contain further instructions as to when to open the others."

The first telegram read:

> Dearest Bonnie, please go to a balloon launching north of the train station.
>
> Love, Wallace.

It was 1889, and a balloon debut would be extraordinary for the small town of five thousand. But the weather was unusually pleasant for February in Texas. No winds were blowing. It was as if a false spring had emerged from the dullness. It was perfect weather for a balloon event.

So Bonnie and Jenny had their driver lead his horses to the affair. They were curious as to why Wallace wanted them to go to something he shouldn't even know about—since he was currently in New Mexico. When they were a hundred yards away, they could see and hear the commotion. People had gathered.

A team of men filled a silk globe with hydrogen gas (fumes resulting from an acid-to-zinc reaction). Above the balloon was a net with multiple ropes hanging down, and it connected the balloon to a glorified picnic basket. It was a type of balloon used during the Civil War. It had been used to get a *birds-eye view* of enemy military strength.

Bonnie suddenly recognized the pattern on this particular balloon. It was the one her father rescued during the war and stored in their attic in New Mexico.

Concho Folks

What in the world is Father's old balloon doing in San Angelo? thought Bonnie, as they looked on. They noted that, remarkably, the fabric was holding the lightweight gas completely. It looked like a safe craft.

Meanwhile, in the Cuchillo Negros Mountains of New Mexico, her father was teaching the gold, silver, and zinc *mining craft* to Wallace, a man with whom Bonnie had fallen in love. It was most strange for the balloon to be in San Angelo when the men and her mother were in New Mexico. She began to get suspicious—but Bonnie was highly distrustful of everything, including her own marriage and niche in the world.

Bonnie had been born with two club feet, and even though her wealthy parents had intervened with good health care, she still walked awkwardly—with a severe limp. Bonnie felt limited and ugly. She suspected Wallace married her only for her money.

Jenny, on the other hand, had no problems with being self-confident. She had moved to San Angelo with her husband many years ago. Bonnie's parents had insisted that Bonnie live with Jenny for a while in hopes that some of Jenny's self-assurance would rub off onto her.

So for several months Jenny had been *talking her up* and confirming that Wallace didn't just love her for her inheritance. Bonnie believed Jenny most of the time. But Bonnie frequently let fear and doubt creep into her psyche.

Bonnie frowned as she reflected on the events of the past months.

When they got to the site, a man named Marco motioned for them to come to the basket. He said, "Mrs. Fife, I would be honored to lift you into the basket for your eventful ride."

She looked at Jenny, who had a naughty smile on her face. "Jenny, what's going on?" pleaded Bonnie.

"You are going on a ride, Bonnie! Open the telegram with a two on it."

I love you. Have fun on the flight. Wallace

With severe apprehension, Bonnie allowed herself to be lifted into the basket. There was a stool to sit on. Marco handed her a compass, whistle, binoculars, and water canteen. She opened her parasol and sat down. *What in the world?* she thought.

The basket was tied to an extremely long rope. The other end of the rope was around a large, hand-reeled winch. The winch was bolted to large springs which in turn, were bolted to the wagon bed. Four horses would lead the wagon-anchored balloon. Bonnie soon became slightly airborne.

The crowd cheered *goodbye* as the winch began to unwind more rope, letting her ascend higher into the sky. Jenny yelled, "Rise up and seize the day, Bonnie!"

The anchor wagon took the lifted balloon with Bonnie along the railroad tracks until merging with the Bronte Road. All along that stretch of the trip she used her binoculars to see the telegraph line and train tracks leading to Ballinger. The view was amazing.

A bugler in the wagon announced their approach to some homes along the road. People came out to greet her. Bonnie enjoyed herself. *But where was this thing taking her?* She couldn't help herself, so she decided to open telegram number three while they were on Bronte Road.

I know you feel inferior to everyone because of your feet. You may think I'm embarrassed to be seen with you. I am not. I am proud of you. Please know that I married you because I love you, not for any other reason. Please come to Sugar Loaf Mountain.

Wallace

Looking in the direction the horses were going, she saw a mountain in the distance and finally realized what was going on. Wallace knew that she dreamed of climbing a mountain.

Is this a trick? What good would my legs be for that kind of adventure? she thought. *Will I just stand at the base of that mountain? How can he say he loves me, when he just wants to rub my fantasy in my face? He knows I cannot climb the mountain with my handicap!*

Her thoughts were interrupted as she remembered the catalyst of this humiliation.

At her home in Hot Springs, New Mexico, is a mountain called Kettle Top Butte. Wallace and her dad hiked the four hundred feet of it. Afterwards, when asked why they did it, Wallace said that being in the clouds was a gift from God.

He arranged the New Mexico trip, knowing that Bonnie would not physically be able to go. His remarks afterwards to the family were breathlessly descriptive. The entire summary hurt her feelings. *Why should they have enjoyed the vision I've had for myself?* she thought. The memory of that incident disturbed her.

But the balloon trip continued north for an hour as she angrily remembered that event.

Along Bronte Road, the bugler had no reason to blast a greeting, as there were no homes out in this wilderness. But he belted out *Amazing Grace* anyway to scatter the sheep and cattle below her.

Her bitterness was subdued somewhat by the sea of brown grass swaying gently to the breeze. It was as if she was on a ship and the grass was her ocean. She enjoyed the sights immensely. She never had the urge to blow the whistle or shout out for fear.

On the contrary, she felt very close to God. For a time, a large cloud cast a shadow over the travelers. Bonnie felt as if she was in the safety under the shadow of God's wing.

But distrust came back to break her peace. "Why would a man find me attractive? I cannot dance. I cannot run to greet him. I am moody and judgmental. I abhor him because I know he is just acting. I love him, but we can't be together," she sobbed to herself.

With that, she threw down the three telegrams. The papers fluttered to the south. She began to feel trapped in the basket of the balloon.

She blew the whistle as loud as she could. *If only I had someone to talk to*, she thought. *I want to get down and take one of the horses back to Jenny.* Her mind was racing.

The men stopped the wagon. The balloon came to a standstill. The trumpeter began to play the Scottish song *The Water is Wide* which caused Bonnie to cry. The winch did not pull her down. Time went by slowly as she grieved her perceived failing marriage and life. "Cut the rope and let me drift away," she shouted without notice.

Since they wouldn't cut the rope, she then began to untie the rope that secured the basket to the wagon.

But Marco shouted, "Mrs. Fife! Direct your binoculars to the mountain we're coming upon."

She stopped untying the rope and did as Marco suggested. Without the rattling and bouncing of the wagon, it became clear that another trumpet was playing in the distance. She set her sight on Wallace playing his instrument while standing atop the mountain.

He was a sight for sore eyes. *What is he doing in Texas five days early… and on a mountain at that?* she thought.

Her heart leapt from her frame as the men and horses were very quiet. Eventually the slight breeze brought the tune *My Bonnie Lies over the Ocean* to her.

"Wallace!"

With her spirits lifted, she told Marco to drive on, keeping Wallace in her sight. He quit playing and waved at her while holding his binoculars.

When they were finally at the base of the mountain near Wallace's horse, Marco led Wallace's horse up the hill. Then he manhandled the rope tethering Bonnie's basket. As the horse and rider climbed the mountain, the rope became longer and parallel to the slope.

Eventually Marco was at the top—as was the balloon's basket.

When Bonnie's basket was steady on the ground of the mountain top, Wallace lifted her out of the basket and said, "I knew you always wanted to climb a mountain, and this was my solution to the situation."

He set her down on the quilt and knelt beside her. "I've missed you so much! Being without you has been horrible. Please never leave my side again." He kissed her. "I promise to love you forever, my Bonnie."

"Oh, Wallace, you really do love me."

"Bonnie, of course I do. I always have."

"I love you, but I have had reservations about your love for me," she replied.

"I love you, and God will redirect your suspicions, if you let Him!"

In the background, the basket jostled as Marco's horse slipped downhill a bit. The balloon was the couple's mode to San Angelo.

Apparently, the steepness of the mountain and tension on the rope was too much for the horse—for very long.

So Marco suggested that the event be cut short. For if not, they were about to lose the rope's diagonal position, as it naturally wanted to be in a vertical position.

So they packed up and both got into the basket. Marco let loose of the rope, and the balloon drifted upward. Lots of kissing and hugging occurred inside that basket.

Eventually the winch lowered them, and they were given a lunch basket that had been in the wagon all along.

Then back up to a secure height they drifted, and the wagon set off to go back to San Angelo.

Bonnie and Wallace were very much in love.

And with God's help, Bonnie would trust Wallace for the rest of her life.

CHAPTER 25

1890 Wilbur

D anny was something of an odd duck. He'd never had a friend. He was a fourteen-year-old who could talk to his parents for hours about rocks and minerals.

The little family lived near Water Valley, Texas. The secluded nature of the countryside made Danny's geology books, his only friends.

So far in his life, excursions from home had been only to San Angelo and Fort Concho. Outings might be the highlight of most kids' lives, but not for Danny. The only reason for going to town was to get more geology books. Danny was a bit narrow-minded.

Near his home, the second cotton gin of the county was erected on the North Concho River in 1890. His parents had an idea. It was time for Danny to grow up.

They talked to Mr. Dweedle about Danny working at the brand-new gin. He was hired. There'd be less reading for Danny, during gin season.

When Danny came home from his first day of work, Mama and Papa asked him how the time had transpired.

"Well, I'm really too tired to talk about it. But Wilbur really got on Mr. Dweedle's nerves today," said Danny.

"What did Wilbur do?" asked Papa, thankful that *Danny* hadn't gotten on anyone's nerves.

"Well, he made fun of Mr. Dweedle's very shiny head and the way he whistles to himself," replied Danny.

"I'm sure Wilbur just had first-day jitters. But more importantly, did you do your job correctly?" asked Mama.

"I unloaded cotton the whole day. You would have been proud of me, as I only spoke about geology a dozen times to the other fellas," boasted Danny.

Mama and Papa looked at each other, for they had warned Danny that morning to stay quiet about his extraordinary hobby. They were about to say something when they saw that his nose was in his books once again.

"Son, you know that we told you about talking so mu—" started Papa, but Danny interrupted.

"Roses are red, and violets are blue. The smell of the outhouse reminds me of you," Danny shouted at his papa.

Mama was aghast. Danny didn't know this kind of vulgarity. What had he learned at his simple job? Suddenly Danny's possible *rock-and-mineral* lecture was the last thing on his parents' minds.

"Where did that come from?" Mama asked.

"Wilbur," was Danny's response.

"Well, maybe Wilbur should get fired for insulting you like that!" she said.

"Oh, he didn't say it to me. He said that to Mr. Dweedle at the river's waterwheel," Danny said.

Before the next day of work, Mama told Danny to avoid Wilbur.

But upon arriving home that evening, he rudely barged into the house and then went straight to his books.

"Don't you want some supper, son?" Papa asked.

"Roses are red, violets are blue. God made me handsome, what happened to you?" Danny shouted at Papa.

"Now listen here, son, you can't insult me like that," he said, as he started taking off his belt.

Mama intervened. "Was that Wilbur's poem?" she questioned.

Papa didn't care the origin. He just wanted to teach Danny a lesson about consequences.

"Wilbur said a bad word today," exclaimed Danny, as he darted around the cabin. A moving target is hard to hit.

Papa and Mama yelled together, "Don't say it out loud!"

"We were cleaning the sticks and rocks out of fifty pounds of cotton today. Wilbur kept calling his mother a 'word' all day long."

Danny whispered the *word* to Papa, whose eyes turned as big as eggs.

"You are never to say **that** in this house again," retorted Papa.

"Can I recite the poem he made up about his mother?" Without waiting, Danny recited the rhyme. "Roses are wilted, violets are dead. Sugar bowl's empty, same as your head."

Mama cried, "What kind of family is raising Wilbur? We must put an end to Wilbur's job."

Wednesday, Papa followed Danny to work to speak with Mr. Dweedle about Wilbur's influence on the young employees. But he chickened out at the last minute. He thought about Danny becoming a man, and how a papa interfering would ruin things.

When Danny came home from the gin Wednesday, his parents expected the worst. But there was no mention of Wilbur. Danny just secluded himself with his books, as he'd done his whole life.

Later, Mama hesitantly asked how the day had gone.

"I learned how to bale cotton," Danny replied. "And we sacked a lot of cotton seed today."

Then, from nowhere, he added, "Roses are red, here's something new. Violets are purple, not so much blue."

Surprised, Mama asked if that was one of Wilbur's poems. Danny said, "No. It's mine."

As Mama and Papa were drifting off to sleep that night, Papa said, "If all goes well with this brief cotton-gin job, Danny can start to work full time at the livery stable—away from Wilbur."

This was said in the tiniest of cabins near the river. Little did they know that Danny could always hear his parents' whisperings.

Danny wasn't too sure about working the rest of his life.

So, on Thursday and Friday Danny quoted *Horrible Wilbur* several times, much to the dismay of his parents.

But Mama had a plan. There was to be a picnic at the church on Sunday to celebrate the opening of the new gin.

Confused by their son's behavior that week, Mama planned to talk to Wilbur or Mr. Dweedle or both of them. Papa wanted her to stay out of it. But Mama just couldn't stand having Wilbur ruining her Danny.

At the Sunday picnic, Mama looked for a stranger in the community who would most certainly be Wilbur. But she knew everyone there. She couldn't see anyone who could possibly be Wilbur.

Finally, Mama went to Mr. Dweedle.

"I see that obnoxious Wilbur was unable to attend today," Mama said to him.

Mr. Dweedle said, "Everyone from the gin is here today."

"Who's Wilbur?" he asked.

CHAPTER 26

1892 Her Words

"Would you please let this gentleman sit at your table?" asked the cook of a San Angelo restaurant. Annabelle and Karen Wendler nodded as a superbly dressed, slim man bowed to them.

"I think I recognize you as a childhood friend at the adobe schoolhouse of Ben Ficklin. Do you remember me, Ron?" asked Karen.

He scrutinized the odd pair of women. The younger of the two had a braid and was freckled. But Karen, the elder, was a picture of female perfection. Young Annabelle handed him a note after he was seated and had ordered his supper. The note said:

I am my sister's slave.

I am a child whisperer.

I don't recognize you, but

Who knows what I might discover?

The note drew a curious expression from Ron.

"Please excuse my sister. The flood ten years ago gave my Annabelle such a fright that she no longer is able to audibly speak. You see, we lost our baby brother and mom during that rampage of water," Karen said.

"I haven't seen you since that flood, as my family joined my grandfather in Fort Worth—because of the devastation. I am sorry for your losses," he replied.

"Yes, well, we have yet another loss just recently, which is why we are here, away from our home in Temple. Our alcoholic father just passed away from cirrhosis of the liver. We are here to settle his accounts and bury him," she explained.

He gave his condolences, then was handed another note:

Sis and I have made an existence.

Her dime novels, I complete them.

I have the pen, and she has the thoughts.

The readers, we mislead them.

"What kind of dime novels do you write?" he asked Karen, after he read the poem.

"Oh, I love stories of adventure such as *The Independent Woman* or the *Indian Kidnapping* or *The Valiant Hero*," she replied. "I dictate the stories to my sister as they flow freely from my imagination. She records them in a binder, which I mail off to the publisher."

"I remember your vivid thoughts from when we were ten at Ben Ficklin. You got in so much trouble every day. You were sent to the corner with a *dunce* hat frequently. Why were you like that?" he asked.

148

She pondered the question as they ate their meals. "I never liked school. It was so hard. Spelling bees were the worst. The only subject I loved was arithmetic. I know I seemed to be a bad girl, but really, I've just been misunderstood."

"Annabelle here knows me and helps me," she finally replied. "But tell me what you do, Ron. Where has your life taken you?"

"I am also a writer, but not fiction, as you—rather, I write political essays for the *Fort Worth Weekly Gazette*. My life has been there since the flood, and I can truthfully say that I've been successful in my writings."

"But you know—I never really got over my infatuation with you, my dear."

Another poem from freckled Annabelle said:

> Ron loved Karen, Karen loved Ron,
> Even though they were both only ten.
> The flood took their love, my brother, my voice.
> One writes in a cold, lonely bed.

Rod chuckled. "Now, Annabelle seems to think that you had a crush on me ten years ago. Tell me, Karen, that it is still true."

"Oh, Ron, you were treasured by all the girls of the school, so dashing and proper, you were. Yes, I loved you and was so relieved when I found out that you had survived the flood. Imagine my disappointment when I discovered you'd moved away, without a note or any goodbye."

"Here, here my dear—I had no way of communicating with you— but you were definitely on my mind for quite a while," he replied. "But my grandfather's strict Republican ideas were thrust upon my father, brothers, and me—for better or for worse. Then I just forgot my preflood affiliations. I'm so sorry, my dear."

"Republican? You mean that you write Republican-based essays for the Gazette. I had no idea that you were of that shrewd political persuasion."

The next note to Ron said:

> If Karen could vote, her pessimism denotes
> That she'd choose to be Democrat.
> You a Republican, that's what you're publishin.'
> Future marriage! The chance is fat.

Annabelle watched the two former friends give each other the *stink eye.* She was left out of the loop, as usual, because her inability to speak always set the tone that she was stupid.

Karen generally had a way of ruining the possibility of a husband for both herself and Annabelle. And since Annabelle was now sixteen, she was afire with severing her ties with her Karen.

But Karen required Annabelle. The younger most likely would never be totally free of Karen's hold.

Having finished their meals, they drank their tea and ate their dessert in an uncomfortable setting.

Annabelle handed Ron her last poem to him.

> The honest truth would set Karen free.
> This is what I have thought of.
> If they come too close, she flees from the men
> To make them each her lost love.

Then Annabelle left the table to deliver a sweet poem of thanks to the cooks.

Meanwhile, Karen began to scribble in the binder something that she suspected would dampen—even more—his enthusiasm toward her. Upon handing over the torn binder page with her name and address, Karen got up to leave the table.

The note said, *Krane Wnelder of Tepmel, Texsa*

Ron was shocked.

Ron caught up to Annabelle when she returned from the kitchen, saying, "It appears to me that you do more than just transpose Karen's dictation."

Annabelle gave him a sly smile and left with her sister.

-The End-

Concho Folks

Description

You will find twenty-six stories in this book of almost one hundred human characters. In one sitting you will fondly embrace one story's characters, setting, problem(s) and solution(s). You might find yourself liking some stories and disliking others. But by reading this book you will know something about the Concho Valley and the nation as a whole—in the late 1800s.

During that time period, West Texas was becoming urbanized. Therefore many of this book's stories depict pleasures and struggles in and near the town of San Angela—called San Angelo, beginning in 1884.

The author diligently tries to depict the times—its customs, social arrangements, physical geography, towns and politics—in a relevant manner. Enjoy the fictional literature!

The author also collects photos of the region and its historical settings. She loves to cut and paste these snapshots of time—into original creations—which she then traces. A traced sketch is assigned to each story. Enjoy the traced sketches!

About the Author

I am a retired science high school teacher living in San Angelo Texas. I love writing and illustrating short stories and poems. My blog can be viewed at: http://pamsliterature.com/ Climbing Devil's Courthouse Mountain—once called Sugar Loaf Mountain—is on my bucket list. My husband and I enjoy visiting our five sons and their families, gardening and cooking for gatherings.

APPENDIX

Can you match the characters of these stories to the words below?

Addiction

Alcoholism

Arachnophobia

Asperger syndrome

Bad luck

Blindness

Club feet

Color blindness

Compassion

Compulsive liar

Deafness

Delusions of grandeur

Dyslexia

Entrepreneurship

Fascination with pranks

Homosexuality

Klinefelter syndrome

Mental illness

Narcissism

Obsessive Compulsive Disorder

Pareidolia

Personification

Savant

Selective mutism

Supernatural

Superstition

Unplanned pregnancy

Unreliable narrator

Go to my website's home page http://pamsliterature.com/and scroll to the bottom of the page. Click on various tabs in "SEARCH MY TAGS" to see if you are right.

Made in the USA
Middletown, DE
28 February 2020